LIVES ENDANGERED

ENCHAINED HEARTS, BOOK 3

EVE NEWTON

Lives Endangered

Enchained Hearts, Book 3

Copyright © Eve Newton, 2020

1

~Cassie~

The world came rushing back as I opened my eyes.

I was on the sofa, placed there by one of my men after Rex had told me that he used to be a contract killer.

I sat up suddenly and saw Alex with his hand on my feet. Lachlan was perched on the coffee table, his elbows propped on his knees and his fingers steepled as he stared at me.

Rex was nowhere to be seen.

"Where is he?" I demanded, leaping up off the sofa. "Where the fuck is he?"

"He left," Lachlan said quietly.

I spun around to face him, absolutely furious. "Of course, he did," I spat. "That's what he does, he fucks off when things get rough."

"I don't think…"

"Save it," I said with so much venom, he backed off.

I sighed, running my fingers through my hair, my other hand on my hip. "Fuck this," I muttered. "You two are in so much trouble. Why did you lie to me?"

"I asked them to," Rex said from behind me, having

somehow opened the front door so quietly, I didn't even hear him.

I took a deep breath and turned to face him. He was ashen.

It struck me how haunted he looked, how…*scared.*

"A contract killer?" I hissed at him as he shut the door as quietly as he'd opened it. "Are you fucking joking?"

He shook his head slowly. "I wish I could tell you that I'm joking, but it's the truth. I wanted to tell you after we got close, but I was afraid of losing you. I couldn't lose you…"

"You didn't trust me enough," I snarled.

"I couldn't with this. Everything else, but not with this, because losing you would devastate me, Cassandra. I couldn't take the risk."

"And you two?" I spat out at Lachlan and Alex, who were hovering close by. "What's your excuse?"

"Don't blame them," Rex spoke for them. "They found out by accident not that long ago and I asked them not to say anything."

"How long is 'not that long ago'?" I asked quietly, dreading the answer.

"Last year," Rex said quickly, and my heart plummeted.

"I see," I said again and felt like crawling into a hole. "How could you, Rex? How could you do this?"

"That bastard came into our home with the sole purpose of hurting you," he snapped at me suddenly. "I don't care what you think of me, but there is no way I was letting him leave here alive to potentially hurt you or *our daughter* again." He approached me, his fists clenched, his face angry.

I wanted to back away, but I forced myself to stay still, lifting my chin a bit higher to show him I wasn't afraid of him.

I didn't know if I was. I hadn't had time to think about it properly yet.

"I don't blame you for Rob," I said quietly. "If he had taken a step in Ruby's direction, I would've killed him with my bare hands. It's…it's the rest…" I shoved my hand into my hair and realized how that sounded.

What a fucking hypocrite.

"I wish I could take it all back for you, Cassandra, I do. But I can't, and I'm not even sure that given the time again, I would make a different choice. You know what a dark place I was in when we met. You brought light to my life so think about what I was like before." He glanced quickly at Lachlan and it was like a punch in the guts. "I was in a dark, scary place," he whispered. "I had no thought for anything I was doing. All I wanted was something to take me to the next day, the next week. A *reason,* however warped and sick, to not kill myself."

I gulped.

It took everything that I had not to go to him.

"Are you done with it?" I asked quietly.

"Yes," he said quickly. "I was done before we even got serious. You were starting to make me *feel* and I couldn't carry on with that life."

"You were feeling guilty?" I choked out.

He nodded, swallowing visibly.

"They were bad people," Lachlan piped up in the silence that followed. "He didn't do anything wrong."

"He *killed* people!" I shrieked so loudly, they all cringed.

I closed my eyes and took a deep breath, tightening the belt on my white silk robe. "Rob was different," I clipped out. "I understand that. He kidnapped me, made me sit there while his friends jerked off with their creepy eyes on me, stripped me naked and bathed me, came really close to raping me…"

I trailed off, wishing that I hadn't revealed all that right now. I didn't want to open my eyes and see their pity. I didn't think I could bear it.

I turned my back on them and opened my eyes to stare at the coffee pot instead. "I need time to think. Don't you *dare* leave again, do you hear me? We are over if you step foot outside of this apartment before I come to a decision."

"A decision about what?" Alex asked, the fear in his voice making it shake slightly.

"On how the hell I'm supposed to live with this," I said and stalked out of the room, down the corridor and into Ruby's room.

None of them would follow me in here, I knew that. It was late and she was fast asleep.

I quietly dragged the rocking chair over to her crib and curled up in it, watching my little girl sleep. I relaxed my shoulders and my jaw that had been so tightly clenched during that awful confrontation.

Could I forgive Rex for his past? If I forgave him for killing Rob, surely, I had to. One was the same as the other. Many, many times over. But I was a hypocrite if I said I didn't forgive him for things he did while being so lost, so alone, so…traumatized. I knew that I brought a shred of happiness into his life. I knew that I anchored him. Me and the other men. I also knew that not forgiving him for this would take that away and he would be lost again. Perhaps this time for good.

I sighed and rested my head on the back of the chair as I rocked back and forth, the weight of this decision heavy on my heart.

2

~Alex~

The clock ticked slowly. I was sitting at the kitchen counter; Lachlan was working on his laptop at the coffee table and Rex was sitting in the armchair, pulled up to the window so he could stare silently out over the view of the city.

It was a maudlin silence. None of us had said a word since Cassie disappeared into another room. What were we supposed to say? I couldn't think of anything, so I'd guessed, neither could they.

I flicked the playing cards one by one, onto the countertop just for something to do with my hands other than pour another scotch into the empty glass in front of me.

Flick. Flick. Flick.

I didn't know much more time passed, but I'd had another glass of scotch and when I looked over, Lachlan had fallen asleep on the sofa. Rex was still staring out of the window.

I stood up, scraping the stool slightly.

Lachlan woke up with a start. "Where are you going?" he asked, rubbing his eyes. "You'd better not be leaving."

"I'm going to find Cassie. I need to speak to her, make sure she's okay."

"Leave her," he instructed me. "Trust me. She prefers to work through things on her own."

I gritted my teeth, unusually pissed off by his thorough knowledge of her. I stared at the floor and he went back to sleep.

Deciding to risk it, I snuck out, down the corridor and pushed open the door to Ruby's room quietly. I saw her curled up in the rocker, fast asleep. I smiled, pleased that I knew she would be in here. It was a small win, but a win, nonetheless.

Her eyes opened and she looked at me, yawning. "Hey," she whispered and stood up, creeping over to me and taking my hand. I took this as a good sign.

She led me out of Ruby's room and down the hall to our bedroom. She closed the door quietly and turned to face me.

"Are you okay?" I asked the stupid question that was on my mind.

She chuckled. "Yeah, okay is about where I'm at now."

"That's good," I muttered, feeling like an idiot. She still made me so nervous sometimes. She was definitely way out of my league and I still felt it. "I'm sorry for lying to you. We thought it was best until we figured out a way to tell you."

She heaved a sigh. "I get why you did it. Rex had no one he could count on. Not even me, it seems. But you've developed a relationship with him. He trusts you enough to keep a secret this huge from the world. From me," she added quietly, her gorgeous green eyes lowered sadly. "I'm glad that he has that. I'm glad that he has you and Lachlan there for him."

"Do you forgive us?" I asked quietly.

"Yeah," she huffed. "You anyway. Lach will take a bit more time. He's way more complicit in this than you are. I know that for a fact. I know his face too well. Dickhead." She smiled softly.

"And Rex?" I dared to ask.

"I'm not discussing that with you before I've talked to him. He still here?" Her eyes flashed with warning.

"Yes," I quickly reassured her. "Okay, I respect that."

She nodded and then pulled me closer, tilting her head back for a kiss. But before my lips touched hers, she said, "If you ever lie to me again, about anything, I won't be so forgiving."

"Understood," I said seriously and then lightly placed my lips on hers.

She deepened the kiss, giving the go ahead to claim her mouth, letting me know that we, at least, were good.

I cupped her face and wished that I could take her to bed, but she'd always shut me down in the past for one-on-one.

I sighed and pulled back, my hard-on bulging in my jeans.

I watched her as her eyes went sultry and she flicked open the robe to show me her gorgeous body, naked underneath.

I raised an eyebrow at her. "Yeah?" I asked eagerly.

"Oh, yeah," she laughed. "We are doing this. I'd decided already to give you guys a break and let you have some alone time with me."

"Starting with me," I chuckled. "How lucky."

"Make good use of it," she replied, drawing me closer by pulling on my shirt. "It's been a while since it was just the two of us."

Too long.

I didn't hesitate to wrap my arms around her and kiss her again as if it was our last day on earth. Sweeping my tongue over hers in a kiss so sensual, I felt my dick pushing against my pants, needing to reach her.

I brushed her robe off her shoulders and picked her up. She wrapped her legs around me as I turned us to the bed and walked over to it. I dropped her lightly and got to work removing my shirt as she started on my pants. They dropped around my ankles and I kicked them off with a quiet laugh. She smiled and gripped my cock in her hand, gently jerking me off a few times before she opened up and took me in her mouth, sucking me long and hard.

"Fuck," I breathed, pushing my hand into her hair. "You are so beautiful."

She worked me over, grazing her teeth down my length, licking my tip, sucking me all the way into her mouth until I was ready to burst.

"My turn," I grunted eventually, needing her to stop. I didn't want to come in her mouth. I wanted my dick firmly in that sweet pussy before I let go and drenched her.

She giggled and let me go, opening her legs so that I could drop in between them to lick her pussy. She fell back to the bed as I saw to her, pulling her legs over my shoulders as I tongue fucked her into a climax that shook her whole body as she gasped silently, clutching at the coverlet. I smiled up at her, glad that she didn't alert the other men to our activities. I was afraid that she would tell them they could join in and our time would be over.

I slipped my fingers inside her. She was so wet I groaned softly and twisted my fingers, making her arch her back and writhe on the bed, her nipples like bullets.

I let her legs drop from my shoulders and, keeping my fingers inside her, I loomed over her and took one of those ripe nipples in my mouth, gently biting down on it.

I removed my hand from between her legs and braced myself. I had to take her. Knowing that I was going to be the first and last lover she would take in this moment, made me groan out loud as I sank into her soft, wet heaven and thrust gently, just feeling her encase me.

"Fuck, Cassie. I love you," I murmured.

"I love you, Alex," she whispered back and then it went savage.

She dug her sharp, pointed nails into my back and scraped me harshly as I slammed into her so hard, I thought she might break in half. I pushed on her hips so that I could get deeper inside her as I devoured her mouth. She wrapped her legs around me and clung to me with her thighs. I knew she was going to roll us over so that she could ride me, and she did.

"Oh, yes!" I gazed up at her perfect tits, with their intricate daisy chains etched around her nipples as they bounced in front of me. I sat up and sucked one into my mouth, grinding my teeth over it roughly as I knew she liked.

She gasped and her pussy clenched around my dick, making me groan and unload into her.

We fell back to the bed, panting and giggling and for a split second I thought she would be taken from me, but she wasn't. She snuggled up to me and I pulled the coverlet over us.

"Thank you," I muttered into her hair as I kissed the top of her head.

She swatted me gently. "No thanks. We are married, we can fuck when we want to."

I let out a loud laugh that I smothered into the covers. "Too fucking right," I chortled but then sobered up. "I mean for everything. For being so forgiving over keeping you in the dark. It was a mistake and one I deeply regret. It ate at me every day."

She sighed, but she didn't move away from me to my relief. "It's done," she said eventually.

I truly felt that it was in that moment. For me anyway. We had resolved it between us. I just hoped that it was as easy for Lachlan, although I doubted it after what she'd said.

"About what *you* said about Rob," I ventured after a beat. It tore a hole in my heart to hear what she went through.

"Forget it. It's over," she almost snapped at me and I shut it, not wanting to ruin the moment between us.

She heaved a huge sigh and muttered, "I'll tell you if I need to talk about it. Okay?"

"Done," I agreed, glad that she'd at least acknowledged that it might become a problem further down the line.

Then we settled into an easy silence and she soon fell

asleep in my arms and I relished every second of this alone time with her.

It was only as I was dropping asleep myself that I remembered something. Something so bad that I haven't mentioned to anyone, something that is going to cause Cassie to be so angry with me, she might never forgive me.

Ella.

Fucking Ella and her baby that she insinuated with her actions was *mine*.

I was screwed.

3

~Lachlan~

I woke up with a start as I rolled over and fell off the sofa. I landed in between it and the coffee table and rubbed my head.

"Fuck's sake," I muttered and looked at the clock. It was still early but light out.

Rex was still by the window, but Alex was gone. Probably went to sleep in an actual bed.

I stood up and stretched, yawning and made my way down the hallway to find Cassie. She wasn't in Ruby's room, as I'd expected so that meant she was in our room.

With Alex.

With a grimace, I pushed open the door to see her feeding Ruby, a sheet wrapped around her naked body. Alex lay next to her, out for the count and also naked.

Great.

I'd figured she'd do her usual thing and want to be left alone, so I'd left her. Alex went to her and got lucky. Real lucky.

They'd fucked one-on-one.

Something that I'd *never* had with her.

I pushed the anger aside as she looked up at me and smiled. "Morning," she said and looked back at the baby.

"Hey," I huffed at her. "You still pissed?"

She chuckled. "With him?" She gestured to Alex with her chin "Nah, not so much. With you? Yeah, little bit."

I scowled at her and sat on the bed. "Why me?"

"You knew the longest and actively went out of your way to lie to me. Alex…he just got in the middle of it. It's obvious." She shrugged.

"I didn't *actively* go out of my way. Rex asked me to keep the secret, so I did. He needs someone on his side, you know…"

"Yes, I do know and I'm glad that he has you and Alex. I just wish he knew that he had *me* as well."

She looked so sad when she said it, I felt the guilt rear up.

"He knows," I said quietly. "He does, but this was something he wasn't risking his relationship with you on. He couldn't and I don't blame him. If it weren't for Rob, I know you wouldn't be taking it as well as you are."

She threw me a death stare, but she knew I was right. She sighed and muttered, "I know."

"So not pissed at me anymore?" I asked with my usual casualness.

"'spose," she gritted out. "But no more, Lach. I can't take it. Especially not from you. If he's keeping anything else from me, I need to know."

"You'd have to ask him that," I said, holding my hands up. "But I hear you. I'm glad all of this is out in the open."

"Me too. How is he?" she asked, lifting Ruby up to her shoulder to pat her back.

"Silent and staring. You need to go out there."

"I will." She placed Ruby in the small crib next to our bed.

When her hands were free, I stuck my finger in the sheet at her tits and pulled her to me. "Alone time?" I asked.

"Yes, and I'll get there with you too. But I want it to be spontaneous. I don't want it to be planned out. If it's three weeks from now when the moment is there for us, then so be it."

I nodded because what else could I say. "We've never…"

"I know," she smirked at me.

My phone buzzed in my back pocket and I pulled it out with a frown. "I'd better get this," I said, waving it at her and standing up.

At her raised eyebrow, I added, "Eliza."

She frowned at me and I realized she had no clue who I was talking about. "The *new* new club manager. She kicks ass."

"Does she now?" she murmured, looking less than impressed.

"Yeah, you know, with the staff and clients…"

"Why did you hire her so soon after hiring someone else?" she interrupted me.

"After the…thing…I didn't trust him." I frowned at her.

"Oh," she stated with pursed lips. "I want to meet her, of course."

"Of course," I said, wondering where the spark of jealousy had come from that I saw lurking in her emerald depths. "I should…" I held the phone up again.

She waved me off and I disappeared as she climbed out of bed. I knew she was going to talk to Rex now, so I took my phone into the office and hit redial.

"Hey, baby," Eliza purred down the phone.

"Hey," I replied. "Everything okay?"

"Yeah, just something I need you to see," she said, switching from flirty to business when I didn't take her on. She was a firecracker. Flaming red hair, enormous tits that she preferred to encase in red leather with her nipples popping out, an ass you could bounce a coin off and pouty red lips that had more than one of my security guys begging to shove their cock in between. I knew she wanted me to beg her too, but that wasn't happening. I was completely a one woman-two guy man. No room for anyone else at my inn.

"I'll be there a bit later," I said. "Unless it's urgent?"

"Video taken from the second playroom. I'm iffy on whether this is a violation of club rules."

"Have they left already?" I checked my watch. It was 7.00am. While we were open 24/7, it was a pretty quiet time.

"Yeah, but he's a regular. He'll be back."

"What does *she* say?" I asked, wishing that I didn't have to ask these questions. I should've been there, making sure those assholes stayed in line. Some of them didn't appreciate Eliza taking over, what with being a woman and all. I expected this kind of push back from some of the more hardcore dicks that darkened my door.

"Becky reckons it's above board, but…*I'm* not sure," she said angrily, pissed off that I was questioning her. "Do you want me to do this job properly or not?"

"Of course, I do," I said, knowing that she was fiercely protective of the girls. It was one of the reasons why I'd hired her. "I'll be there soon."

I ended the call and chewed the inside of my lip. If I left here now and all hell broke loose, I would never forgive myself if Rex walked out, or worse, if Cassie pushed him out. I needed to be here to mediate. My home life was way more important.

The club would have to wait.

4

~Rex~

I sensed Cassie approach me with caution. I didn't blame
her. She probably thought I was a monster. I *was* a
monster. I didn't think I would ever be able to look her
in the eyes again. She handed me a mug of coffee, black like
we both preferred.

"Hi," she said softly.

I took the mug from her but didn't take a sip. I leaned
forward and placed it on the low windowsill. "Hey," I
muttered.

"Did you get any sleep?" she asked.

I shrugged. She knew I didn't sleep much anyway; she
was making small talk because she was nervous.

"Rex," she murmured, "Look at me."

I didn't want to. I didn't want to look into those beautiful
eyes and see what she thought of me.

It took everything that I had to raise my eyes to hers and
hold her gaze.

She was smiling, tightly, but it was a smile.

"I didn't leave," I croaked out lamely, just for something to
say in the silence that fell.

She snorted. "No, you didn't. I'm impressed."

"Cassie…"

"Let me speak, please," she interrupted me. "I can't judge what you did in the past any differently to what happened to Rob. It makes me a hypocrite and I know you had your reasons for doing what you did. I had no idea that Uncle Teddy was *that* shady, though." She chewed her lip in consternation.

I snorted but didn't say anything.

"They were bad people?" she asked quietly. "All of them?"

I nodded. "Apparently. I didn't know at the time." Full disclosure. "The first one was the drunk driver who killed your aunt."

I watched as her face went ashen. She licked her lips and placed her coffee cup next to mine on the windowsill. "Oh," she muttered. "They were all killers?"

I nodded. "In one way or another."

It made all the difference to her. I saw it in her eyes. The trepidation she had over forgiving me disappeared, to be replaced with resolution.

"I see," she said and then came closer to me, pushing me back into the chair and crawling onto my lap. "I forgive you, Rex. I'm sorry that you felt that you couldn't come to me. I want to be here for you, but you have to let me. You *have* to let me in. Please. No more secrets."

"I can do that," I said to her, knowing that if she knew the worst possible thing about me and still loved me, there wasn't anything I couldn't tell her.

"I love you," she murmured and pressed her lips to mine.

"I love you, Cassie," I said, shoving my hand roughly into her hair and claiming her mouth with mine. I needed her, desperately. "Punish me, Mistress. Punish me for my sins."

"All in good time," she muttered and that on its own was punishment enough. She'd denied me and it would torture me until she decided to lay her hands on me.

I pulled back from her, respecting her wishes when there was a loud knock on the door.

I frowned at it, wondering who the hell it could be at this hour.

Cassie leaped off my lap and strode over to the front door. She stared at the video intercom with a fierce scowl.

"Who is it?" I asked her, coming up behind her and peering over the top of her head. "Oh, her," I scoffed, as I looked at Suzanne waiting impatiently on the other side of the door.

"Go away," Cassie said into the intercom.

I forced down the chuckle at Suzanne's furious face on the little screen. If looks could break cameras, ours would be toast.

"Cassie!" she called through the door, banging on it. "We need to talk. Now!"

"It's early, Mom, come back later. Or better yet, call me." Cassie gave me a grin, riling her up on purpose.

"It's about Rex," Suzanne spat out. "I'll happily say it from where I'm standing, but who knows who will come by and overhear me?"

Cassie and I exchanged a look. We were in the penthouse. It was the only apartment on this floor. No one 'came by' unless they were expected.

Usually.

"She's not going away," Cassie whispered to me. "We're better off just letting her in."

I grimaced at her. I had a fairly good idea what Suzanne was here for. I hadn't given in to her request to sign away my parental rights of Ruby. Her threat of telling Cassie about me was now moot. What would be the harm? "Fine," I huffed and leaned over Cassie to open the door.

"What is it, Mom?" Cassie asked, folding her arms over her chest as Lachlan swooped in behind us and Alex stumbled into the sitting room, still half asleep, and naked to boot.

Suzanne's eyes swept over her son-in-law with far more

interest than Cassie was happy with. She snarled in her mother's face, drawing her attention away from Alex, who finally realized that he was naked in front of company and ducked back out of the way. Derek was also present, but he just glared at us all in a menacing silence.

Suzanne's eyes landed on me and I knew that I was correct about her motives for coming here.

She licked her lips and adopted a predatory look on her face. "You've been a naughty boy, haven't you, Rex?" she drawled. "Do you want to tell Cassie all about it…or should I?"

I looked at Cassie and she looked back at me with raised eyebrows. Her eyes were furious, but not with me. She spun back to her mother and spat out, "Whatever game you're playing here, save it. I already know *everything* there is to know about Rex." She straightened up as Suzanne's eyes widened in surprise and then hardened, knowing she'd lost her only leverage. "Now, if you don't mind, it is early, and we haven't had breakfast yet. Leave, and don't bother coming back."

I heard Cassie's rapid breathing and saw the slight shake of her hand. I took it in mine, and she calmed down.

"She said get out," I said, giving Suzanne a death stare that Derek was not particularly fond of.

He growled at me, but I turned that same glare onto him. He didn't back down, nor did he approach. He knew by now not to mess with me.

Suzanne licked her lips and gave us all a cool stare back. I could see the wheels turning and knew that this wasn't over. She was plotting and we would see the fallout from this conversation very soon.

5

Cassie

"Can you believe the nerve of her?" I shrieked as Alex sauntered back into the room, towel slung around his hips in a really sexy way.

"Cassie," Rex said quietly and took my hand to turn me towards him. "I have to tell you something."

My hammering heart nearly stopped at those words. "What is it?" I asked stiffly, pulling my hand from his.

"Nothing that *I* did," he said with a small smirk which quickly disappeared, "something *she* did."

I blinked. "What did she do?" I whispered, not sure if I wanted to know.

He sighed. "She came here today to tell you about me because I didn't do what she asked me to."

"What was that?"

"Don't interrupt him and he'll tell you," Lachlan chided me gently, taking my hand and leading us over to the sofa. "Perhaps we should sit while we have this conversation."

I sank onto the soft sofa and looked at Rex as he lowered himself to the coffee table. Alex slipped in next to me, his arm going around me, his head nuzzled close. He was unusually needy this morning and I wondered if it had anything to do with our one-on-one sex last night.

Lachlan sat down next to Rex and put his hand on his leg.

A sudden bolt of lust drove its way through me, and I felt myself go damp. Ever since Ruby had been born, we'd barely been together in that way. It was all I could think about. I licked my lips and tried to focus on what Rex was saying.

"...sign away my parental rights."

"What?" I asked, having been thinking about taking his pants off and not what he'd been saying. "What are you talking about?"

He gave me a frustrated look. "Your mother. She threatened to tell you about my past if I didn't sign away my parental rights to Ruby."

It was like a punch to the guts. I was suddenly extremely focused on this conversation. "Why? Why would she do that?"

He sighed again. "She said that once you inherit your entire fortune, she knows that you will be working around the clock, like her father did and not be there for Ruby growing up. She wanted me to give up my rights and convince you to do the same eventually, so that she could become her guardian. It is *clearly* only because Ruby will be set to inherit everything once you are ready to pass it on. I told her to go to hell, obviously."

I'd stopped breathing as he said all of this. In spite of everything he'd said about my bitch of a mother, only one question came to the forefront and I dreaded the answer.

"Did you only tell me about your past because of this?" I choked out.

His eyes went hard, his lips pressed tight together. "I understand why you've asked me that so I won't take it personally," he gritted out, "but the answer is no. I wanted to tell you because you needed to know who you were living with."

If it weren't for his death grip on Lachlan's hand that I'd only noticed he'd taken in his a moment ago, there is no way he'd have remained so calm while saying that. He was inches away from flipping out.

"I believe you," I muttered, realizing that I did and that it didn't matter anyway. The truth is out, but I'm thankful it came from Rex and not as a blindside from my mother.

He relaxed, but his eyes were a black storm of emotions that told me he was still very close to the edge of that ledge he teeters on every minute of every day.

I leaned over and took his hand, bringing it to my lips and kissing his knuckles. "I love you." I murmured, and it reassured him enough to relax as much as Rex could.

"So, she wants my daughter because she will lose everything when Grandaddy gives me my full trust," I focused on what was important.

He nodded.

"Un-fucking-believable," Lachlan spat out. "That's it, Cassie. I'm putting my foot down. That bitch is done here. No more."

"Oh, you don't need to convince me," I said angrily, not at him but at her. "She is a fucking lazy, manipulative parasite. She will *never* get Ruby. I would never abandon my baby. How could she think that I would?" I burst into tears mortified that my own mother could think that I was such a heartless monster.

All of my men fell on me to reassure me that there was no way Ruby was going anywhere.

"Enough!" I said after a few minutes of this. "She *is* done here. Tell security to never let her or that massive idiot into the building again!"

"Oh, more than done," Rex growled. "About time."

I fixed him with a cold stare. "All right, I get it, you've hated her from the start. But we are here now, okay?"

"Okay," he said, a small smile playing on his lips.

"Good." I stood up and loosened my robe, letting it drop from my shoulders and onto the floor.

Rex's eyes raked over me, dark with desire. I climbed into his lap and kissed him, putting every ounce of love that I had for him into it. He returned it, fisting his hands into my hair and tugging just this side of roughly.

Lachlan was quick to join in, reaching out for my nipple, twisting it harshly before he dropped his hand to my pussy, that I was rubbing against Rex's jeans, making his cock grow. To my surprise and delight, he ignored me in favor of placing his hand over Rex's bulge and squeezing gently before he flipped his hand over and slipped two fingers inside me, his thumb going to my clit to press down gently.

I threw my head back and rode his fingers as Rex held onto me, latching onto my nipple to suck it gently before he ground his teeth over it and bit down. I cried out at the spike of pain, but I wanted it. Needed it.

Lachlan moaned as I creamed his hand, pushing two more fingers inside me for me to use to bring myself pleasure.

Alex stood up next to Lachlan and dropped his towel, showing me his hard cock as he took it in his hand. I licked my lips inviting him to push it in between them for me to suck.

I gasped when he didn't but took his pleasure in his own hands.

"This is just for you," Lachlan murmured.

I shook my head. I wasn't a selfish woman, I wanted to share the love with my men, show them how much I loved them.

"Yes," Alex insisted and continued to jerk himself off as I watched.

Oh, I would enjoy this. They all knew that I loved watching a man climax. It would bring me to the point of my own with Rex tugging on my nipples and Lachlan's fingers deep inside me.

"Ooh," I moaned, casting my gaze to Lachlan, who couldn't keep his eyes off Alex.

Rex concentrated solely on my aching buds and when Alex started to pant, and tug quicker on his huge cock, I knew it was imminent. I put my fingers over Lachlan's thumb to get him to push harder on my clit as I rose up slightly to slam myself down onto his fingers, my eyes riveted to Alex's dick.

He groaned loudly as he came, jets of cum streaming out to splat on the hardwood floor.

I moaned in response and clenched forcefully, feeling the rush of my orgasm race through me.

"Fuck, yes," Lachlan muttered, his eyes on me, watching me come all over his hand. "I want to lick you."

I nodded my consent, wanting this too. He lifted me off Rex's lap and lowered us to the floor with me on top of him. He dragged me to his face, and I settled over him, close enough so that he could tongue fuck me as well, but not smooshed down so that I'd suffocate him. I giggled as I knew he wouldn't complain about death by pussy. In fact, it was probably the way he wanted to go out of this world.

"Love you, Daddy," I murmured to him, looking down into his eyes, that went wide before they hooded in suspicion and then understanding.

He took his mouth off me for long enough to say, "Be still, little girl, while Daddy fucks your pussy with his tongue."

I shivered on top of him, my aching nipples puckering even more as my clit twitched. Those words coming from him were exciting, thrilling, dangerous. I needed it. I needed more.

I needed to feel the lash of a whip on my back and looked to Rex to do it.

"Whip me," I ordered him. "Do it while Daddy has his tongue in my pussy."

Lachlan moaned into my sopping wet haven, as Rex shook his head vehemently.

"I'll do it," Alex croaked out and before I could be shocked or stop him, he was off to the bedroom to procure the instrument that would bring me the greatest pleasure, at the same time as giving me that bite of pain I craved.

I couldn't wait.

6

~Alex~

I fumbled in the back of the closet with no idea what to grab. The one with several dangling bits on it or the riding crop or even the one that looked like an actual whip.

"This one," Rex said, leaning over me and handing the dangly bit one to me. "Better for an amateur as it's softer on the ends."

"Thanks," I muttered and took it off him.

"Why did you offer?" he asked.

"She wants it and you refused," I hesitantly pointed out.

"I don't want that with her anymore. She is my Mistress," he said, folding his arms over his broad chest. "Have you got what it takes to do this?"

"I think so," I said, feeling a bit embarrassed.

"Don't hesitate," he advised. "Lift your arm up high enough to get some swing, but not too high and bring it down quickly, but not hard."

I gave him a look. "Not helpful," I gritted out.

He smirked at me. "Don't worry, I'll show you." He

turned to check on the sleeping baby and then he walked back out of the bedroom, so I followed.

Cassie was just coming again as we approached her. Lachlan was doing an amazing job down there. Her eyes were glazed over from the pleasure.

They went straight to the object in my hand and smiled. "Cat o' nine tails. Good choice," she murmured.

I beamed at her, glad to have a name for it now and taking full responsibility for this even though Rex rolled his eyes at me.

"Stand here," he instructed me, pointing to a spot near where Cassie and Lachlan were.

I did as he said and then got a surprise when instead of taking the whip off me, he stood behind me and gripped my arm tightly. He was actually going to show me how to do this. I felt my cheeks go red, but when he placed his other hand on my hip, and nestled in behind me, I lost that feeling and grew warm for a whole other reason. I'd never thought of him in this way before. He was a fucking god, sure, but I never looked past that like I had with Lachlan. I didn't think he'd wanted it, so I was happy to leave it. At that moment, I got the impression that he wasn't averse to the idea, but maybe needed more time. Kinda like I did.

"Like this," he murmured in my ear and lifted my arm up and then brought it down so the ends of the whip lashed Cassie across the back.

She arched it and cried out, but they weren't cries of pain. It was ecstasy.

"Yes," she panted. "More. Harder."

Rex took my arm and lifted it back and this time brought it down that bit harder.

She shuddered and came in Lachlan's mouth as we lashed her back. I was enchanted with her. I didn't think I would get off from someone whipping me, but she was loving every second of this.

Rex stepped back from me and I figured I was on my

own now. My palms started to sweat. Lachlan picked her up and moved her off him and she immediately went onto all fours.

"I've been so naughty," she murmured to me. "Punish me."

I blinked rapidly, and did as she said, hoping that I did it just as Rex had and didn't hurt her.

As the whip connected with her back, she gasped and then moaned. "I need dick," she panted. "In me. Now. Rex, get over here."

He didn't need asking twice. He had his pants down and was on his knees with his dick in her before I'd even lashed her with the whip again. She took Lachlan in her mouth and they each fucked her hard and fast while I flogged her repeatedly.

"Oh, fuck, yes, Suits," Lachlan panted as he fucked her mouth. "You are turning me on real good." He grunted and shot his load into Cassie's mouth, ramming his cock down her throat one last time before he withdrew.

Rex followed quickly, as did she and I dropped the cat o' nine tails to the floor and dropped to my knees to kiss her sweetly to take the sting out of what I'd done to her. I swept her up into my arms as Rex let her go and caressed her back gently.

"Does it hurt?" I murmured to her.

"No," she replied, shaking her head. "It was perfect. Thank you."

I kissed her again, swishing my tongue around her mouth, tasting Lachlan's come and then I just held her for a moment.

"No more secrets," she muttered and stood up. "I'm going to check on Ruby and take a shower."

I nodded at her as she left the room, feeling the guilt rear up in me. I had to find out once and for all if Ella did have my baby or if she was messing with my head. I hoped that it was the latter, because if it wasn't and I *had* fathered a child with her, I knew that Cassie would hit the roof, especially if I didn't come clean about it soon. I had to act fast, but I had no idea where to start.

That is until I looked at Rex and knew that he had the means to gain this knowledge quickly and quietly.

"We need to talk," I muttered to them as I bent down to pick up my discarded towel. "It's serious."

They both looked back at me and nodded, knowing that we couldn't talk here. I was surprised, even though I shouldn't have been, that they both just accepted it. No questions asked.

Yet.

I knew once I told them what had happened, they would have plenty; the Lord knows that I did. But I needed them to help me figure this out and get the facts first before I confronted Cassie with this. To do so with only suspicions and accusations could make this a whole lot worse than it had to be.

7

~Cassie~

As I got ready that morning, I felt as happy as I'd been in a long time. It had been a few days since I'd found out about Rex – not to mention what my mother had been plotting – and I knew that I'd made the right decision in trusting Rex. He was different now. Not vastly different, but he was more open to cuddling with both me and Ruby, he was less brooding, and he smiled more. Plus, there was that whole thing brewing between him and Alex. I was *very* interested in seeing what they would do about it. I'd seen the little glances, the brush of their hands over the coffee pot. It was new and exciting.

Rex was as relaxed as I'd ever seen him. I truly felt that we'd turned a huge corner in our relationship and that he had within himself.

Things could only get better from here. The threat of Rob was gone, my mother's toxicity had been rid from our lives and our little family unit was thriving.

The only dark spot that *I* had was this Eliza character. Since Lachlan had told me about her, I'd heard them laughing on the phone late at night when she called him to 'report in'. I was sure that she made up half the stuff she had to "report" just so she could talk to him. I didn't know why it was bothering me so much. Apart from the obvious of her being a manager of a sex club, it was probably because I hadn't met her yet, so my imagination was running wild. I intended to rectify that today.

"I've got an errand to run," I told Aurora, who was giving Ruby her mid-morning bottle, "and then I'll be going into the office for a couple of hours – max. I'll be back before five."

She nodded at me, keeping her eyes on Ruby. It was so obvious how much she loved our little girl and that made me happy as well.

"Uhm, about that guy…" she ventured after a beat.

I froze. "Rob?" I croaked out.

"Yeah, is he…I mean, is it safe…"

"Oh," I said with a sigh of relief. "Yes, perfectly. He won't be hurting anyone ever again where he's gone." I twirled my finger at my head, and she got my meaning that he'd been put away for being an insane, gun-wielding maniac.

This was the story and we were sticking to it.

"So, can I take Ruby to the park?" she asked.

"Yes, of course." I smiled at them both and then bent to kiss Ruby's little head. "Enjoy yourselves. I'll call later to check in."

Aurora nodded and then I stepped into the elevator. Alex was already at work; Rex had a job for a client and Lachlan was…at the club. At 10am. I wasn't amused by this. He'd left at 4am because of some trouble or another and he hadn't returned home yet, just a quick voicemail while I was in the shower to say he'd be a few hours yet.

I didn't think I'd catch him up to no good. No way. I trusted him. I did not trust *her*.

I exited the elevator at the lobby and slipped into the car waiting at the curbside for me. George, my driver, was quick to pull off and soon we were around the corner from *Corsets & Collars*.

I felt a pang of nerves as I got out of the car, telling George to stay and that I wouldn't be too long.

I was let in immediately by Stan, head of security and Aurora's boyfriend.

It was dark and quiet, although it was open.

My heels clacked on the wooden floor as I followed the sound of laughter into the main bar area, where I found my husband on top of a ladder, his hand in the venting system, with a very sexy, barely dressed woman looking up at him and laughing at something he'd said.

"Lachlan?" I called to him, trying to keep my tone steady. I was feeling lightheaded all of a sudden. It wasn't like I'd found him on top of her, pounding away, but I did feel like I'd walked into something.

"Oh, hey, Cas," he said, dragging his arm out of the venting and then wiping his hands on the cloth that the woman held up to him. "Everything okay?" he added with a frown as he climbed down the ladder.

"Uh-huh," I muttered and waited for an introduction, which came as he saw me looking at her.

"Cassie, this is Eliza. Eliza, my wife, Cassie," he said, coming closer and then bending to give me a kiss.

"Hello," I said coolly, clutching the handle of my purse as Eliza crossed over, flashing her exposed nipples to us. Her top was a tiny black leather thing with nipple holes. Her skirt literally skimmed her ass. She had ripped fishnets on and spiked heels that you could kill a man with. Her flaming red hair was a waterfall around her face and shoulders, and her pouty lips were slashed with a vibrant red that I was secretly jealous of.

I adjusted the jacket of my white work suit, suddenly feeling so frumpy, I wanted to escape this room and never come back.

How in the hell could Lachlan look at her and then look at me, only a couple of months after having a baby, and think I was sexy?

I drowned in the insecurity that swamped me and I gulped, wishing that I hadn't come here.

"Hey, baby," Eliza purred at me. "Lach has told me *all* about you."

"Oh," I practically spat. "I've heard absolutely nothing about you."

She raised her perfect eyebrow and looked at my husband. "Oh, really?" she murmured and that was it. I was lost in a sea of jealousy that I had never encountered before.

"Excuse us," I barked out. "I need to speak to *my husband*. Alone," I added.

"Sure thing, sweetness," she chirped and with a waggle of her fingers, she left us alone.

Lachlan's eyes were on me, shrouded with concern. "Are you sure you're okay?" he asked. "You look like you're about to blow a gasket. Or two."

I only just stopped myself from snapping and asking him if he was sleeping with her. I clenched my hand into a fist and forced a smile on my face. I wasn't demeaning myself and showing him that I didn't trust him, but he wasn't getting away with this lightly either. "You didn't say she was a hot piece of ass," I tried to say as casually as possible.

He chuckled and relaxed. "Who, Eliza? Nah, not my type." He turned from me and headed to the bar, clearly not realizing that I knew it was a lie. Who did he think I was? Some idiot he'd picked up in a club for a one nighter? I was his best friend of over a decade and his fucking wife.

"Sure," I sneered, "because 'sexy as sin' isn't anyone's type."

He spun at my tone and immediately came to me, taking my hand. "*You* are my type, Cas. Yeah, the guys fall over her, but *I'm* not interested. You believe me, don't you?" He looked panicked all of a sudden and I realized what a dick I was being. Of course, he wouldn't be interested in her. Not only was he in love with *me*, he was also in love with Rex, and he cared about Alex. He would never jeopardize our relationship for anything, not even to get his dick wet with his sex-on-legs club manager.

"Of course," I said, relaxing as he pulled me to him. "I was just surprised by her, that's all, and you've been here ages. You're meant to be spending more time at home." I pouted at him and all was forgiven.

He grinned and kissed me. "I know," he sighed. "But there was this thing, and then the air con broke and sweated out half the clientele. I was trying to fix it when you arrived."

I forced myself not to ask what the 'thing' was. I still didn't trust Eliza. I intended to watch my husband's back for him because he was a big flirt with everyone, but maybe she was taking it the wrong way. But I had to trust him. I *did* trust him.

"What're you doing here anyway?" he asked, leading me over to the bar.

"On my way to the office and I wanted to see you," I said coyly.

"Well, don't let me stop you from dropping by. Especially when you look as ravishing as you do." He leaned down to kiss me, and I accepted the compliment with a happy sigh. He lifted me up onto a bar stool, and I knew that *our* alone time had just dropped into our laps.

8

~Lachlan~

I plunged my tongue into my wife's mouth, suddenly feeling a bit nervous. This was the first time that we were going to be together alone, which sounded ridiculous, but was the truth. I ran my hands up the outsides of her thighs, under her skirt.

She grabbed me by my t-shirt and deepened our kiss, wrapping her legs around me. I knew she didn't care that the club was still open and that anyone, including Eliza, could walk in on us. That only made it more exciting for her.

I brushed my fingers past her pussy, feeling soft lace and then plucking the fabric away so that I could touch her properly.

She moaned as I plunged my fingers inside her once and then withdrew them as I pulled back from our kiss, to push them between her lips. She sucked them enticingly. I was bursting in my jeans. I needed to release my cock immediately.

Her phone buzzed in her purse, but we both ignored it as she sucked my fingers clean and nipped at my fingertips.

I grinned at her and took my hand back, placing it on the back of her neck. "I'm nervous," I laughed quietly.

She snorted in that way that was so sweet. "Me too," she confessed with lowered eyes, biting her lip. "Daddy."

"Uhn," I groaned as her phone continued to buzz away, stop for a moment and then start up again. "Ignore it," I told her as she frowned and reached for her purse.

She drew back and rubbed my enormous hard-on through my jeans. I sighed contentedly and then her phone stopped and mine started in the back pocket of my jeans.

We exchanged a look, the fear slicing through us. I grabbed it as she unwound her legs from me, and I saw it was Rex. I put it on speaker as I answered. "What is it?"

"I know she's with you, godammit, put her on."

"You're on speaker," I informed him.

"You need to come quickly," he said urgently.

We frowned at each other harder. He was outside, that much was clear. "Where?" she asked, leaning closer to the phone.

"Bryant Park," he clipped out.

Cassie's eyes went wide and then filled with so much fear, my blood ran cold. "Ruby?" she croaked out.

"She and Aurora were supposed to be here. They aren't and Aurora's phone is switched off," Rex said, his tone going softer as he spoke directly to her. "Get here now!" he added, practically yelling and hung up.

"Jesus," Cassie whimpered and almost fell off the stool as she grabbed her purse.

"Everything will be fine," I crooned to her, steadying her as we headed straight for the exit. She was trembling as I quickly told Stan I was leaving and to let the air con repairman in when he got there.

I bustled Cassie into the car and told George to step on it.

She'd gone quiet. Silent and still, her bottom lip quivering every now and again. "We don't know anything is wrong," I pointed out. "You know how Rex is…"

She looked at me, so scared, I pulled her to me. She collapsed against me and nodded. "Yeah," she said, but that was it.

George let us out as close as he could and, grabbing my phone to call Rex, we ran through the park.

"Where are you?" I asked as he picked up.

"In front of you," he barked and then I saw him and Alex rushing over to us.

He grabbed Cassie and crushed her arms as his eyes bored into her. "Have you heard from her?"

She shook her head. "No, I knew she was coming here. How did you know?"

"I called her earlier and she told me she was coming. We arranged to meet right here. I didn't want her and Ruby alone…"

I gulped as the fear on his face scared me. He genuinely believed that the baby was in trouble.

"Please find them," Cassie whispered, and it was his undoing. He completely closed off and he was back to the cold, dark creature I met all those years ago. He pulled away from her and she let out a cry as she must've seen it too.

Alex took her in his arms and murmured to her as I grabbed Rex by his arm and dragged him further away. "Start at the beginning," I said to him and his black eyes focused on me as he recounted everything that had happened.

"So, it was half an hour from when you called her to when you arrived, and they weren't here?"

"Yes," he stated. "Anything could've happened to them."

I gave him a furious look. "You need to stop that right now," I hissed at him. "Cassie needs all of us to be positive. This could be nothing. She might have wandered off walking Ruby and her battery died."

"She wouldn't stand me up," he hissed back. "We…we…"

"You what?" I asked suspiciously, my tone low.

"We meet up regularly," he muttered. "It's the only time I get to be her father. Her *real* father."

I reared back from him and folded my arms. "You don't feel you can do that with us there?" I asked incredulously. "What are you embarrassed or something?"

He grabbed me by my t-shirt and growled into my face. "Of course not, you asshole. But I feel that when we are all together, I can't see her as *my* daughter." He let me go with a sigh and he lost the chilly exterior. "I know that you and Alex love her as much as I do and see her as your own. I don't want to barge in and be her only father. So, I use this alone time with her to just be her dad." He choked back a sob and I felt like the biggest douche on the planet.

"You don't have to pretend with us," I chided him, drawing him closer to me. "You *are* her dad. Alex and I are cool with that. Of course, we adore her, but if you want us to step back, we will." It hurt me to say the words, but I knew that I had to.

"No," he growled at me. "I don't want that. We are a family. All of us. I just…forget it. We need to find them."

I tabled the conversation for now, but it wasn't the end of it. I suddenly felt hollow. Rex had Ruby, Alex might have that Ella bitch's child and there was me, not even having had one-on-one sex with my wife.

I sank into a pit of despair, only to be kicked out of it by Rex as he flung his arms around me, in a very rare occurrence of initiating contact.

Cassie and Alex came over. She was calmer, but Alex had that effect on her. He was as cool as a cucumber, but authoritative with it. Not cold like Rex. He was now ordering us around like a dictator as Cassie fumbled trying to keep up with his instructions.

"The police!" she cried when she could get a word in. "We need to call the police!"

Rex paused and looked at her as if the idea hadn't even occurred to him. He was so used to dealing with shit on his own, in his own way.

"If we can't track her down in an hour, then we will," he

said eventually, which was a huge give in for him. "She might have lost track of time and her phone battery died. That's why you need to get back to the penthouse now with Lachlan and Alex and I will carry on looking here. Okay?" He said it so gently, as he took Cassie in his arms and kissed the top of her head. "Okay?" he added urgently.

She nodded and I took her hand.

Rex murmured to me as we turned to leave. "Look after her."

I nodded grimly. In those three words, he conveyed everything that he was feeling. He was convinced that Ruby, and possibly also Aurora, had been taken. He didn't want to involve the police because he was waiting for the ransom call to come through.

We walked quickly back to the car in silence. Cassie was shaking and my hollow feeling was getting worse. I knew in my gut that Rex was right, and this day was only going to get worse before it got better.

9

~Cassie~

I t had been two hours since Rex had called us and there was still no sign of Ruby and Aurora. I'd gone past panic and into something that I've never felt before, not even when I was locked away in Rob's warehouse. I'd called Grandaddy the second we got home to ask what he thought we should do. He and Grandma Ruby had come straight over and convinced me not to call the police.

"If they ask for a ransom, we'll pay it. Simple," he'd said. "Doesn't matter how much, we'll pay, and it will all be over."

The fact that everyone thought that they'd been kidnapped was not good for trying to keep my hopes alive that they would walk in the door any second now with a plausible explanation.

Lachlan was trying his best for me, but he wasn't the one I needed with me right now. I needed Alex. Lachlan was too positive about things. It wasn't a fault, but I needed a realist. Someone who could be gentle but tell me the facts. Rex wasn't that guy either. He was the opposite of Lachlan, doom and gloom man, straight in with the bad news with no cushioning.

Lachlan was currently sitting with Grandaddy making a list of people he thought would want to do this. Enemies.

We didn't fucking have any, I wanted to screech at them.

Rob was dead and he is the only one I would've considered an *enemy*.

They were talking in low tones as I paced by the landline phone with my cell clutched in my hand. Alex had called a little while ago to say they were widening their search to outside the park. Lachlan had contacted Stan so that he could scour any places he thought Aurora might've gone. I saw Lachlan cast a glance at me and then turned right away from me to mutter something to Grandaddy.

"Who?" I roared at him, knowing that he'd thought of someone who had a grudge. "Who?" I demanded, marching up to him and prodding him on the shoulder.

"It's a long shot…" he started with a sigh.

"Aren't they all?" I shrieked at him, my last nerve snapping and if it weren't for Grandma's arm going around me, I would've fallen to the floor in a sobbing, messy heap.

"Ella," he stated, giving me a wary look.

I gave him a blank one back. "Who?" I asked in confusion. "Who is Ella?"

I saw him roll his eyes at me, even though he tried to hide it behind his hand.

"The stalker, girl," Grandaddy shouted at me. "From the other year!"

My eyes widened. I had totally forgotten all about her. Rex said he'd taken care of it and I'd assumed he'd paid her off as I'd never seen or heard from her again.

"Oh," I muttered with a fierce frown, this suddenly making a lot of sense. She would've needed time to plan this. "Yes!" I said, getting oddly excited about this. "It's her. It has to be!"

"Wait," Lachlan said. "Let's just calm down. There are other names on this list."

"But none of them have ever stalked us before, have they?" I asked.

"Not that I know of," he said, standing up and taking me in his arms. "But you know Rex…he might have pissed someone off…" He trailed off and gave me a look.

"That fellow is as brusque as they come," Grandaddy piped up. "But this Ella girl needs looking into. Do we know where she is now?"

"Yes," Lachlan said. "She is with Teddy."

"What?" I asked incredulously. "Are you fucking joking?"

"Uhm," Grandma started at my expletive.

"Keep your enemies close, sort of thing, I think," he said, turning away, his voice going up an octave.

"What aren't you telling me?" I demanded, pulling on his arm to get him to face me again.

He was saved from answering me by the phone ringing. The landline. I leaped over to it, snatching it up and answering with a shaky voice.

"H – hello?"

"We have your daughter and the nanny," a distorted voice came down the line.

My hand was shaking so badly that I dropped the phone and Lachlan scooped it up and held it between our ears so we could both listen.

"In forty-eight hours, you will have a drop in Bryant Park, you know the place. Three million dollars or they both die."

I let out a sob and then listened to the dial tone as they hung up. "Wait!" I screamed into the phone even though I knew it was pointless. "Wait…" My knees gave way and I dropped to the floor before Lachlan could catch me.

Rex and Alex came barging in then and as Grandma consoled me on the sofa, Lachlan filled them in.

"Why – why forty-eight hours?" I asked, but everyone ignored me.

I stood up, bunching the tissue Grandma had given me into my fist. "WHY FORTY-EIGHT HOURS?" I roared. "Why not an hour? They know I'm good for it, obviously, or they wouldn't have targeted me. Why are they making me wait?"

I knew that my use of first person was selfish and wrong, but I didn't care. Not even when Rex gave me a hurt look briefly before his cold mask fell back into place.

"To torture us," he stated with emphasis, his voice like ice. "They want to torture us before we pay up. This is personal. Very, very personal."

I gulped as we fell into an uneasy silence. Only my grandmother's quiet sobs could be heard over the ticking of the clock on the mantelpiece.

"I'll get the money together," Grandaddy said quietly after what seemed like forever.

"Thank you," Alex said to him, just as quietly as Rex and I just stared at each other.

"Who?" I whispered. "Who is doing this to us?"

He shook his head and with grim determination spat out, "I've got forty-eight hours to find out."

With that, he stormed out of the penthouse and I knew that if he found our daughter in the next two days, whoever had her was dead.

I couldn't have been more supportive of that idea if I tried. I hope he killed them slowly and painfully.

"Help him," I muttered to Lachlan. "But don't get in his way."

He nodded once.

I turned to Alex, and he held tightly onto me as I heard Lachlan leave.

This was going to be the longest wait of my life.

10

~Rex~

I stabbed the elevator button repeatedly, knowing it was pointless, but needing the release of my frustration somehow. If I didn't stab *something*, I was going to stab *someone*, and I wanted to leave that until I found the fucker who'd taken my daughter. Make no mistake, I was going to make them bleed. I was going to make them hurt so badly they'd wish they'd never been born.

"Why are you here?" I snapped at Lachlan as he stood calmly next me in the elevator as we descended to the lobby.

"Cassie wanted me to come with you to help you."

"Don't need help."

"Not with the whole finding and killing. The afters," he said.

I swear I thought I'd heard him stifle a snicker.

"This funny now?"

"No, not at all. I just find amusement in the fact that when you find these assholes, they'll wish they'd never gone through with this idiotic plan to snatch *your* child. I mean, come on, are they fucking stupid or what?"

I turned to glare at him, but he was giving me that lazy

smile that was so damn hot, I stopped being angry with him, at least.

"That's why she sent me," he said and took my hand as we stepped out of the elevator. "So where to?"

"Teddy's," I replied.

He nodded. "You think Ella has something to do with this."

The fact that he phrased it as a statement, didn't surprise me after what Alex told us the other night. Unfortunately, what I'd managed to find out in the couple of days since, especially today, wasn't good news, but I hadn't had a chance to speak to Alex about it yet. I'd called him as I was walking onto the park to tell him to meet me afterwards when I realized that Ruby and Aurora weren't there. He came straight away, but we hadn't discussed the disturbing results that had been confirmed to me only mere hours ago.

"Did you find anything out?" Lachlan asked as we climbed into my black SUV.

"Yeah, but he should be here before we discuss it."

"That bad, huh?"

"We'll talk about it with him here."

He sighed. "Shit," he muttered and then we spoke no more on the drive over to Teddy's estate, about half an hour away.

I impatiently tapped my fingers on the steering wheel as the drive was interminable. When we finally pulled up and got through the gate, we escaped the car and marched through the open front door to where Teddy was waiting for us.

"Boys!" he boomed. "What can I do for you today?"

"Where is Ella?" I barked out. Pleasantries could wait.

He frowned at me. "What do you want with her?"

"Where. Is. She?" I gritted out.

"Being punished for being a naughty little girl. She is locked away in her room. She'll be let out when I decide."

"We need to speak to her. Now," I informed him, not interested in his sex games.

"What about?" He narrowed his eyes in suspicion.

"Ruby has been kidnapped," Lachlan said quietly. "We think Ella might've had something to do with it."

Teddy's eyes went dark. Really dark and he spun around and marched off, leaving us to follow him, we assumed, so we did anyway.

He pulled a key out of his pocket and unlocked a door on the ground floor, at the back of the mansion.

Lachlan and I exchanged a look as we heard a soft cry and realized that the baby had been locked in the room with her.

I was about to take Teddy by the collar and demand what he was doing here, when he shoved the door open and he stormed in with a curse.

We rushed in behind him, but the room was empty. The window on the far side was open, the curtain rustling in the slight breeze.

"Damn her!" he roared, scaring the baby even more.

She was sitting in a playpen, left entirely on her own in a locked room. I gulped and looked at Lachlan. His face was grim. I'd never seen him so angry before on behalf of someone other than Cassie.

"She left?" I snapped.

"Seems so," Teddy muttered. "I'll whip her until she's black and blue!"

He stormed back out of the room, leaving us with the child.

"Uhm," Lachlan said. "Two things. Firstly, if Ella isn't here, it only makes me even more sure she did this. Secondly, we can't leave that baby here. Dude, I need to know. Is that baby Alex's?"

I let out a sigh. "Yeah. The hospital where Ella had her did a paternity test. They matched it to Alex's. She must've had something of his from when they were together."

"Shit," Lachlan muttered. "How the fuck is Cassie gonna take this?"

"We have to get *our* baby back to her first. We need to find Ella," I said coldly and turned away to leave the room.

"No way," Lachlan said, grabbing my arm, stopping me. "We can't leave her here."

"We can't take that baby and hunt down her mother. If she did this, I'm going to fucking kill her. Do you really want her child being a part of that?" I asked him gruffly.

"Well, no, but is leaving her here locked up and alone any better?" he implored me.

I blinked and looked back at the baby.

"She's family, for fuck's sake," he added, and I knew he was right.

I clenched my jaw and reached out for the diaper bag on the dresser. I threw it at Lachlan and then I scooped up the girl, who whooped with delight, and left the room determinedly. I wasn't sure if Teddy would fight us for the child or not.

We aimed for the door and Teddy didn't stop us.

"When you find that little bitch, you leave a piece of her for me," he said with such venom, that even I raised an eyebrow at him.

"Any ideas on where to look?" I snarled at him.

The baby started to cry again, and I passed her over to Lachlan. I didn't have it in me to console her when I was barely hanging on by a thread.

He juggled the baby and the bag but managed to quieten her down long enough for me to hear Teddy growl, "No fucking clue."

"Great," I muttered and then we left, slamming the door behind us.

"What are we supposed to do with her?" I asked Lachlan as he started to strap her into Ruby's car seat. "Got any ideas?"

"Yeah, get in and start driving."

I did as he asked, we were winding our way back into the city, wasting precious damn time.

"We need to get back to the park," I snapped eventually. "There has to be someone who saw something, a camera, anything."

"I agree, but pull up here and I'll be five minutes," he said and leapt out of the car before I'd even cut the engine. He got the baby and bag out and disappeared into a block of apartments, returning five minutes later and sliding back into the car.

"Who lives here?" I asked suspiciously.

"Eliza," he said shortly.

"The new club manager?" I asked. "How do you know her address?" I turned to face him, needing an answer to that before I focused solely on finding my child.

"Her job application form," he snapped. "Now get going."

It wasn't like Lachlan to be so tetchy. I figured it was to do with the kidnap and nothing to do with Eliza.

I hoped anyway.

I stored this away for when Ruby was back safe, and I had time to kick his ass if he was up to anything shady.

We headed back to the park and I did a thorough sweep, finally happening on an old British couple having a picnic, who'd seen Aurora and Ruby on the other side of the park a couple of hours ago with two "dodgy-looking fellows," they'd said.

It was a start.

11

~Cassie~

I watched as Alex put his phone away with a grim look again. This was the second call he'd taken, and it looked like the news was just as bad as the first time. I was still reeling from the news that Ella was living with my uncle. How could he?

I'd just seen Grandaddy and Grandma out, convincing them to go home and that I'd report in with any news.

"What did he say?" I asked quietly.

"They found a lead back at the park. They're following it. That's all I know." He huffed in frustration and I knew then that he wished he was out there with them and not stuck in here with me.

"I'll be okay, if you want…"

"No!" he exclaimed. "I'm staying here with you. I'm not leaving you on your own. Who knows what this psycho wants or will do next?"

This psycho.

I started to tremble again, and an ugly sob escaped that I was unable to hold back.

He came to me instantly, wrapping his arms around me.

"Rex will fix this," he murmured as he stroked my hair. "He will bring her home."

I nodded, my hands over my face. I couldn't bear the thought of my little girl out there without me. I thanked God that at least Aurora was with her, hating myself for that because she was also in danger.

"They won't hurt her," Alex mumbled.

"How do you know? That woman is a complete lunatic!" I suddenly shrieked at him, pulling away from him, blaming him for bringing this woman into our lives. The more I thought about it, the more I'd decided it was Ella that had orchestrated this kidnapping.

I spun around knowing it was unfair of me to blame Alex. She was *my* housekeeper at the same time she'd been screwing him. We'd *both* invited her into our lives. We were both to blame. Me more than him.

"We don't know it's Ella yet," he said carefully.

I turned to him, a vicious snarl escaping my lips. "Don't fucking defend her to me! Rex and Lach said that she wasn't at Uncle Teddy's where she was supposed to be. Don't think I've forgotten about everyone failing to mention *that* nugget of disgustingness, as well. It's her. I *know* it. I can feel it in my gut."

"Okay," he said, coming to me and taking me by the shoulders. "Okay. We'll assume that until told otherwise."

I gritted my teeth so hard, my jaw ached.

My stomach was in a knot, my head was pounding, my heart was breaking, and I had absolutely no idea how to take my next breath without my baby here, safe and sound.

I lost all of my fight and just fell into his arms, crying, inconsolable.

He guided me towards the sofa, and we sat for ages with him holding me, trying to comfort me, until I couldn't take it anymore. I needed action. I couldn't sit here a moment longer without doing something.

"I'm going to find Rex and Lachlan," I told him, standing up and clenching my fists.

He stood up as well. "I don't think that's a great idea," he said carefully. "If Rex finds them…you shouldn't be there."

"You think I can't handle seeing him do what needs to be done?" I asked him, full of scorn. "You think I will stop him from punishing them?"

He shook his head. "No. But I think that *he* won't do what needs to be done with you there. He will be afraid that it'll change how you see him. Don't get in his way, Cassie. It's not a good idea."

I took in what he said. He seemed to be fully on board with Rex punishing those who took our baby. "He knows I accept him and love him," I said quietly. "You can stay here, but *I'm* going."

He sighed. "Of course, I'm coming with you."

I turned and walked down the hallway to our bedroom. I needed to get out of this work suit and into something more suitable.

I threw my phone onto the dresser and stripped off as Alex followed me, also unbuttoning his shirt as he came into the room.

I caught my breath and turned away from him. I rooted through my dresser until I found a black, long-sleeved tee, which I slipped over my head and then headed to the built-in closet for a pair of soft black jeans.

As I did them up, I frowned at the delicate gold Rolex on my wrist and took it off, placing it on the dresser carefully. That's when I felt Alex come up behind me. I looked at him over my shoulder. He was shirtless, the jeans that he'd hastily pulled on were undone at the fly. I turned away as I couldn't look at him like that and not want him.

I drew in a deep breath as he pressed his body close to mine and slipped his hands under my tee, pushing it up until my bra was exposed. He gently tweaked my nipples through the lacy fabric.

"Alex," I sighed, putting my hands over his.

"Ssh," he murmured, his hands dropping to the waistband of my jeans. He flicked open the button and lowered the zipper.

Then he did something that startled me, but at the same time made my heart pound.

He grabbed me by my upper arms and shoved me up against the mirrored closet door. My breasts were squashed up against the cold mirror and I shivered. Alex took my hands and placed them on either side of my head. I turned it so that my cheek was pressed against the chill of the mirror.

"What are you doing?" I murmured.

"Ssh," he whispered again and pulled my jeans down.

His fingers found my clit in the next moment and I trembled against the mirror. He slipped a finger inside me quickly before withdrawing.

"Alex…"

"I said quiet," he softly snapped at me and placed his arm across the top of my shoulders to hold me there.

I gasped as he held me in place, my hands splayed out on the glass. I went damp between my legs; I couldn't help it. He'd gone dominant on me and after the flogging the other morning, it was something that I hadn't dared hope for.

He pulled my hips back with his free hand and guided his cock to my entrance. He shoved in hard, making me cry out. He wrapped his arm around my waist to keep me in place as he pounded into me.

It was inappropriate. It was the *wrong* time for this.

But I didn't stop him.

I let him use me and to my shame, I enjoyed it.

I needed the release I was going to get, or I was going to snap in half with the worry and anxiety and *anger* that was threatening to consume me.

My hot breath fogged up the mirror as I panted, my arousal going off the charts. I came suddenly and quickly. There was no fanfare about it. But it was what I needed.

I turned my head so that my forehead was resting on the cool mirror and stood there while Alex fucked me until he came.

It didn't take long. He was as worked up as I was.

He withdrew immediately and pulled my jeans back up, slapping my ass and turning from me to carry on getting dressed.

My breath was ragged as I reached down to do up my jeans, my forehead still leaning against the closet door. My hands were shaking. I pulled my top down slowly.

I wanted to grin with joy at Alex's sudden turnaround. He was good at being dominant. *Incredibly* good. I don't know where it had come from, but I knew it wasn't just to do with me. *He* wanted it, and I was fine with that. But right now, wasn't the time to celebrate that.

I ignored him as I picked up my phone from the dresser and shoved it into my back pocket, stalking out of the bedroom. Alex followed me out, picking up the key to Rex's black Mustang.

"Do you know where they are?" I asked him, not looking at him as I pressed the elevator button.

"Yeah, I'm tracking Lachlan's phone," he replied, also keeping his eyes averted from mine.

I knew he was keeping his distance because I'd gone cold. But as we stepped into the elevator, he reached for me.

I drew my hand back as if I'd been scalded. The guilt tore through me that I'd taken a few precious minutes to think about myself instead of my kidnapped baby. What kind of person was I? What kind of *mother* was I?

I'd told Aurora to take Ruby to the park. I'd told her it was *safe*. This was all my fault.

I stifled my weep in my hand as we stepped out of the elevator and Alex opened up the Mustang. I stiffly climbed in and as he started up the car, I broke down.

Alex squeezed my knee, but that was all he did, and I was grateful.

He knew that I didn't want or need his comfort.
All I needed was to cry.

12

~Alex~

I placed my phone steadily in the holder and set it to the tracking app that Lachlan insisted we all had. I didn't bother calling him. I didn't want Rex knowing we were coming. He would go ballistic, but Cassie was going to find them whether I was here to help her or not.

Her heart-wrenching sobs ripped through me, but I knew that I had to leave her to cry. She didn't want my comfort. It took everything that I had not to pull over and reach for her. I gripped the steering wheel tighter, gritting my teeth against the agony of worry over Ruby and Cassie's heartbreak.

I took a great risk doing what I did before, especially in the way I did it. Ever since the other morning, I couldn't stop thinking about how it felt to have that kind of control over her. It was intoxicating. I'd always been worried that she would get hurt, but she truly reveled in that pain and it had opened my eyes even more. I could do this for her. She needed it and so help me God, I *wanted* it. Of all the roles that I could play with her, I never envisioned it would be the dominant one. Not after my past.

Yet.

Yet, I'd done it, fucking enjoyed it and wanted to do it all the damn time.

I'd held back earlier. I'd wanted to completely overpower her, but it was perfect the way it was. It was sexy as hell and just what I needed. I was sure she did as well, which is why I did it. If I'd thought otherwise, I would have left her alone and jerked off in the bathroom for my release instead.

As we wound our way through the maze of the city, Cassie's sobs quietened down to sniffles now and again until she went silent.

I cast a glance at her, wishing I could hold her. She looked completely defeated. I'd never seen her look so lost. Not even after Rob. She'd carried on fighting, but it was all because of Ruby. Without her, she had nothing to fight for.

"We're nearly there," I muttered to her and squinted at the phone. They'd been stationary for a while now as we'd made our way towards them. They were in a parking lot, which surprised me.

I turned down the street and then into the practically empty lot. It was getting late, although still light out and we were in a dodgy part of town.

Cassie looked up from her soggy tissue and frowned.

"Where are we?"

I shrugged and spotted Rex's SUV over in the far corner. I pulled up next to it and he wound down the window with a look so fierce, I found myself flinching just a little bit.

"What are you doing here?" he snarled.

Cassie was already out of the car and slipping into the back of the SUV, so I did the same, locking up the Mustang and hoping if we had to leave it for a time it wouldn't get stolen, or worse. It was a beauty of a vehicle.

I slammed the back door closed and Rex turned to scowl at us. "Go home."

"No," Cassie said. "What are you doing here?" She leaned forward, fully composed now, to look out of the front window.

"I was about to call you," Lachlan said. "We didn't want to get your hopes up before we had something concrete, but at the same time, it seemed cruel to leave you in the dark."

"Go on," Cassie growled at him.

"We got a notification on Rex's phone. A tracking signal. For Ruby. Aurora must've planted it, linked it to Rex's phone and activated it as soon as she got the chance."

"What?" Cassie spat out. "Why not just have it on the whole damn time?"

I risked putting my hand on her leg and to my relief she took my hand and gripped my fingers instead of pushing me away.

"Probably because it was a secondary precaution. Rex has Aurora's phone tracked, but of course it's switched off."

"I also had a tracker in Ruby's diaper bag," he said quietly. "But there has been no signal from that all day. I figured it was dumped."

Cassie glared at him. "You had another tracker and you didn't say?"

"What was the point? It was dead!" he snapped back and for the first time ever in their relationship, I saw a flicker of danger in his eyes when he looked at her.

She saw it too and licked her lips. She wasn't afraid, if anything she wanted him that way. It made me feel like a complete dick for trying to be that for her when it was quite clear that she wanted it from *him*. I took my hand back and she turned those livid green eyes on me. It must've been written all over my face though, as she softened slightly and took my hand back firmly, lacing our fingers together.

"Everybody just calm down," Lachlan interjected, his eyes on our hands.

He brought his eyes to mine and I saw the hurt lurking there. He knew we'd been together. I felt bad knowing that I was the only one who'd had one-on-one time with her, *twice*, but it wasn't my fault that I was there at the right time and seized the opportunity.

He gazed longingly at Cassie before he said, "The point is, Aurora had foresight and she's had the means to execute it now. We know they are in there." He pointed through the window to the grim looking building on the far side of the parking lot.

"Then what the fuck are we waiting for?" Cassie yelled and started to get out of the car.

"Him," Rex said, and we all looked to where he was pointing.

A sleek black Mercedes pulled up and Teddy got out. He ignored us as he went to the trunk and pulled out a huge black hold all. He crossed over to us and Rex got out to take it from him, with muttered words. I didn't hear much of what they said, but a question about putting something somewhere. Rex growled back at him and then he climbed back into the SUV, dumping the bag onto Lachlan's lap.

It didn't take a genius to figure out what was in the bag.

I watched as Teddy drove off and then cleared my throat. Everyone was still looking at the bag, except Rex, who was reaching forward to unzip it.

"Uhm," Lachlan muttered. "Do we really need an entire bag full of guns?"

"I don't know how many are in there," Rex countered as he cocked a handgun and shoved it into the back of his pants.

My mouth went dry, but I knew what I had to do.

I held my hand out for one.

Rex glanced at it and then dismissed me. "I'm going in alone," he said as he shoved another gun into the back of his pants and then grabbed two spare magazines, putting one in each pocket of his black leather jacket.

"No way," I said determinedly. "We do this together."

Lachlan nodded and stuck his hand in the bag, pulling out a huge handgun that looked better suited for a hit man than a sex club owner.

I gulped and looked at Rex.

He rolled his eyes and took it from Lachlan, swapping it for a smaller one. Then he handed one to me.

"Do you know what to do with this?" he asked.

I nodded. After I'd been beat up and hospitalized by Rex's ex-pimp, I made sure I knew how to use one. I'd had one for a while, but as time passed, I got rid of it as I'd felt that I didn't need it anymore.

He raised his eyebrow at me and then nodded once. "Let's go."

"Uhm, excuse me," Cassie barked out before any of us could move. "What the fuck?" She held her hand out.

"Err, no," Rex said and then climbed out of the car. "Stay here."

I bit my lip as her temper shot into the red zone. "Why, because I'm a girl?" she yelled at him. "Give me a fucking piece."

He snorted as he bent down to look into the car. "A *piece*? What are you, darlin'? A fucking wise-guy?"

Lachlan barely stifled his laugh of amusement.

I quickly exited the SUV as I knew she was gonna go full Mistress on Rex's ass and he was in for a *world* of trouble.

13

~Rex~

I knew that I'd riled her up. It had been my intention. I knew that there was no fucking way on this earth that she was staying in the car while we went into that building. I needed her focused. I needed her worry to be gone and her anger found. It was the only way she would get through the next few minutes.

Her eyes were boring into mine as I smirked at her and I knew that I'd done what I set out to do. She was furious.

"Stay here," I reiterated and watched as her cheeks went bright red.

I straightened up and gave Alex a half smile. He looked sexy as fuck holding that weapon. I couldn't help the feeling of lust that washed over me.

"Put it away," I muttered to him and he quickly shoved it down the back of his pants, like I had done. I stepped closer to him, needing to feel the heat that was growing between us. "You sure you're okay to handle this?"

He nodded grimly and I felt my dick go hard. I kind of

hoped that he got the chance to point it at someone, I wanted to see it.

Although, as far as I was concerned, none of them were getting anywhere near any dirty work. No, that was my cross to bear. I was letting them tag along so that we could actually get a move on and not stand here arguing the toss about it.

"Give me a gun," Cassie snapped at me, getting out of the car and slamming the door behind her. "Or I swear to the Almighty God, Rex, if you don't do this, I will withhold your Mistress from you *indefinitely*."

"Ouch," Lachlan muttered.

Alex snorted. "I kind of figured the opposite was about to happen here," he muttered.

I gave her a slow, sinister smile, one that I knew would wet her panties. I saw the look she gave me in the car earlier. She still wanted me to dominate her, hurt her, even though I'd told her repeatedly that it wasn't happening. She liked that edge, that danger that came with being with me. She'd known enough about me when we very first got involved to know that I was a loose cannon and she'd got off on it. Still did.

Only now, I was hoping that Alex would take up that role with her. He did well enough the other morning. Christ knows I'd been hard for him as well as my wife when I'd fucked her from behind like an animal.

"No gun for you," I told her. "You have no idea how to use it and you might end up hurting the wrong person."

I didn't say it to be mean, but to be practical.

"No Mistress for you then," she retorted, but shoved her hands in her jeans pocket. She wasn't wearing a jacket and it was starting to get chilly.

"Let's move," I mumbled. This was turning into a disaster, and why I'd wanted to come alone. There was zero stealth about this mission, and I was afraid we would lose our advantage if they saw us coming.

We walked across the parking lot in silence. I was trying to formulate a plan that would keep everyone I loved safe, yet still hurt the fuck out of these bastards that had my daughter.

We entered the building and started up the stairs. There was no working elevator. I went in front and kept Cassie in the middle, Alex and Lachlan came up behind. I was on edge, but my laser-like focus was solely on retrieving my daughter safely; making sure she and Cassie were out of the way and then all bets were off.

I looked at my phone as we got to the third floor of the dingy apartment building. It was dimly lit and there were loud shouts and music coming from all over. I felt a bit better about our lack of finesse. There was no way that anyone would've seen us coming from this apartment, as I'd figured anyway, and as for hearing us, nah, that was definitely off the table as well. This place was a cacophony of noise.

I stopped in front of a door and pocketed my phone. I indicated to Lachlan and Alex to go to either side of me. Cassie stubbornly refused to move, standing right behind me, her chin in the air.

"Move over there," I mouthed to her.

She shook her head at me until I was forced to grab her by the upper arms and move her over to stand behind Lachlan. She gave me a death stare, but it only made me love her even more. I took up my position again and slipping my hands behind me, under my jacket, I gripped the two guns tightly, then I brought my booted foot up and kicked the door in.

It bounced roughly as I marched forward, but I knew instantly that Ruby wasn't there. My heart sank as I saw Aurora tied up and gagged.

I did a sweep anyway, even though Cassie had stormed in behind me like the devil was on her ass.

"It's clear," I sighed as Alex untied Aurora.

"She's not here," she blurted out. "They took her somewhere else. I'm sorry, I tried to go with them, but she kicked me, and I passed out. I'm okay. I came to only a few moments ago and that was there." She indicated with her chin to the flashing tracker on the table. "But she has a message for you."

"What message?" Cassie screamed, scaring her.

"She said that she knows you have her daughter. It's now four million dollars and Scarlet for Ruby."

I blinked. "Scarlet?" She fucking named her child Scarlet. What kind of a psycho was this bitch?

"What?" Cassie shouted out, shoving her hands into her hair. "We don't have anyone's daughter. Who was it? Was it Ella? Silly bitch. Looks like a fucking Barbie doll?"

Aurora nodded. "That's her. I didn't see her until a few minutes before she gave me the message. It was two guys who took us from the park and then a third was here, they were all masked, but he seems kinda familiar." She shrugged. "I don't know why though."

"Son of a bitch!" Cassie screamed and kicked out at the table, knocking it flying across an otherwise barren room. "Was she hurt? Did they hurt her in any way?"

"No, she was unharmed. I fed and changed her about…" she checked her watch, "…an hour ago. She's good for a little bit."

"That's how you activated the tracker?" I murmured, and she nodded.

"Where the fuck is she?" Cassie asked quietly now, the reality sinking in that we'd lost her for a second time. "And who is this Scarlet? Why does she think we have her daughter? And, hello? She has a daughter? Is my uncle the father?" She shuddered.

Lachlan and I exchanged a knowing look and then turned to Alex. He was pale, stricken.

"Tell me," he whispered, getting Cassie's attention immediately.

I nodded at him. "She's yours," I muttered and watched as Cassie went apoplectic.

Alex nodded grimly as Cassie went up to him and

slapped him so hard across his face, she left scratches down his cheek.

"You bastard!" Cassie hissed. "You have a fucking child with that bitch? When were you going to tell me?"

"He only just found out. Literally," Lachlan piped up, a braver man than I, it seemed. "But we have bigger issues right now. This can wait." He placed a calming hand on his wife, and she gritted her teeth, turning from Alex coldly. "Aurora, did she say she'd call us to arrange a swap?"

"S-swap," Cassie choked out. "Where *is* this girl?"

Lachlan ignored her as Aurora picked up a burner phone from the floor where it had fallen when Cassie lashed out.

"She'll call you on this."

"Let's get going then," I said, sweeping an arm around Cassie to get her moving. Lachlan grabbed Aurora by her elbow and fell into step. Alex trailed behind us, reeling from the information that had been so callously handed to him. I felt bad for him, but right now, we had to get Scarlet back from Eliza, pick up the money from William and make sure that we got our daughter back safe and sound.

Then it was my unfortunate burden to get Ella out of the picture. For good, this time, like I should have in the first place.

14

~Lachlan~

As we got back to the SUV, Cassie was distraught. I knew she'd gotten her hopes up, we all had, only for them to be dashed. I steered Alex in the direction of the Mustang, but he was way ahead of me. He gave me a panicked look, but there wasn't anything *I* could say to reassure him. That had to come from Cassie.

I reached out and stroked his scratched cheek. He sighed and closed his eyes.

"Quite the hellcat, our wife, isn't she," I murmured as I leaned over to kiss him lightly.

His eyes flew open. "I deserve worse," he said miserably and then he got into the car and drove off before we'd even discussed what the plan was.

I climbed into the front of the SUV, as Cassie had slipped in the back with Aurora.

As Rex set off, Cassie asked her, "Do you need to go to the hospital?"

"No, honestly, don't worry about me, I'm fine. Drop me with Stan and then make sure you bring your daughter home and make those fuckers pay." A pause. "I'm sorry I couldn't protect her. If you want to fire me, I understand."

"Don't be ridiculous. You did everything you could," Cassie said quietly. "*I* understand if you want to leave us. We have been a source of trouble for you since you started."

"I'm not going anywhere," Aurora stated with finality and that was the end of all conversation until we dropped her off with Stan and carried on pulling up outside Eliza's building.

"Where are we?" Cassie asked.

"Wait here," I muttered and climbed out.

I'd gotten the very clear impression that Cassie was not a huge fan of Eliza's. It was better that the two catalysts that might set her off remained as far away as possible until it became necessary to bring them all together.

Eliza buzzed me in and was waiting with the door open when I got out of the elevator, the baby in her arms.

"Finally," she exclaimed, pursing her lips at me. "Jess is watching the club, but I've gotta get there. It's getting busy."

"I know. I'm sorry. Thank you for this," I told her earnestly. "We'll give you a ride."

"Awesome," she said and grabbed her bag.

She was fully decked out in her BDSM gear and I cringed. Cassie was going to hit the roof, but I couldn't let Eliza go in alone for two reasons. One, she'd had a hold of Scarlet all damn day and who knew what Ella and her goons would do if they knew that, and two, it *was* late, and she needed to get to the club. Jess was competent for day shift, but night was a whole other deal.

As we headed downstairs, Eliza said, "Wanna tell me what all this is about?"

"Not yet," I muttered. "Uhm, Cassie is in the car and she's upset... don't..." I paused, wondering how to phrase 'don't piss her off' without sounding like a dick.

"Don't what?"

"Nothing," I mumbled, taking the coward's way out.

We got to the car and I opened the back door to find

Cassie's eyes riveted to the baby. They pooled with tears as I started to strap her into Ruby's car seat, but we had no choice.

I suppose I could call it lucky that her attention was pulled away from the baby and to Eliza as she opened the other side and got in, squeezing in next to Cassie.

"Hey," she said. "Thanks for the lift."

Cassie's furious eyes found mine and I shrugged. "It's on the way home and she needs to get to CoCo."

She silently fumed at me as I slammed the door closed and hastily got back into the car.

Rex gave me a raised eyebrow, having fully taken in Eliza and her nipple clamps and I gave him a shrug too. What was I supposed to say? She managed a sex club. Was she supposed to turn up in jeans and a tee?

He turned again and frowned at her, which caught my attention, but then his face closed off and he turned forwards and drove off.

"She's a real cutie, this one," Eliza said. "Kinda made me all broody."

I froze as I heard Cassie hiss.

"You're so lucky," Eliza carried on, clearly not realizing that this *wasn't* our baby. Sure, I hadn't stopped to tell her who it was or why she was looking after her, just that we had no one else to watch her. I shook my head at myself. What a fucking idiot.

"That baby isn't mine," Cassie snarled. "My husband's, though? Yes, she belongs to him, it seems."

I gulped.

"Oh," Eliza said slowly. "Sorry, I knew you guys had a kid. Lach didn't say much when he brought her round earlier. I figured…ya know."

"Is that right?" Cassie said, her voice like ice.

"You're really wound up tight," Eliza commented. "Having three guys, I'd have thought you'd be more relaxed." She laughed, but Cassie was silent. "I could loosen you up a bit," she added.

Her voice had gone seductive and I spun around to see what in the hell was going on in the back seat.

I caught sight of Eliza's hand halfway up my wife's thigh, with Cassie glaring at it as if it was a poisonous snake.

"We're here," I croaked out, trying desperately but failing miserably to push away the sudden scene of Cassie and Eliza, locked in a hot embrace.

"Thanks for the lift, sugar," Eliza murmured in Cassie's ear and licked her with a wicked laugh before she got out of the vehicle and Cassie's eyes found mine. I wasn't surprised to see anger there, but I was surprised to find a slight heat, which turned cold as her eyes bored into mine.

I turned away from her and willed my dick to go down. I couldn't get out of the car sporting a hard-on that would put someone's eye out. Cassie would take it all wrong. I didn't care about Eliza. It was Cassie that I wanted to see taking her pleasure from a woman, any woman. I wanted to see my wife tongue fucked as she writhed in pleasure against the silk sheets.

They would be faceless to me. I wanted to see my wife, only my wife.

We finally got home, and Cassie was out of the SUV before Rex cut the engine. He was grimmer than usual, and I knew it had something to do with Eliza.

I scrambled out to get Scarlet and her bag while Cassie stormed past the Mustang that signified Alex was home already, which I'd kind of figured he would be.

I really hoped that Cassie didn't tear his nuts off before he got half a chance to explain. Maybe I was being naïve, but I really thought in that moment that it would make a difference if she knew.

15

~Cassie~

I was out of the elevator as soon as the doors opened. I had to get out of the enclosed space. Alex was sitting on the sofa, his head in his hands. He had his glasses on and his face was ashen which told me he was coming down with a migraine. I wanted to go to him and make sure he was okay, but I was still so angry with him.

"I hope you're prepared to make this exchange to get *my* daughter back," I spat at him and saw him flinch. His eyes landed on the baby in Lachlan's arms and he gulped.

I carried on walking, clutching the burner phone to me like a lifeline. I disappeared into the bedroom and closed the door, crossing over to the windows to stare out over the city.

How did this day end up like this? How did my baby end up being abducted by that psycho bitch?

I heard the door open and close softly.

"Please let me explain," Alex said quietly. "I didn't know about the baby. You know that I had unprotected sex with her, I told you that. I told you it was a big mistake. I didn't think that this would happen. I never knew about the baby. We saw her for the first time in months when you…you'd been taken by Rob. She had a stroller and she insinuated that the child was mine, not with words, with actions…It was confusing. I forgot about it because getting you back was more important, and I only remembered about it the other day. I asked Rex to find out what he could. I guess he found out that the baby's mine. I'm sorry, Cassie."

I blinked for the first time since he entered the room as he uttered those two words. He sounded so lost it broke my heart. I was being a complete bitch about this. I knew it, but I was hurt and angry. Maybe I wouldn't be so furious if I wasn't already in the middle of the worst day of my life.

"You don't need to be sorry," I said, turning to him. "It happened. There's nothing we can do about it now." I cupped his cheek gently. "I'm sorry for hurting you. It was completely uncalled for. I was just…I got my hopes up, you know…"

"Hey," he said, lifting my chin up that had dropped so low. "We all did, and then this bombshell. I wanted to say something, but I knew coming to you with a half-assed idea and nothing concrete would only frustrate and upset you needlessly. I wanted more information before I said anything."

"I get that," I said, knowing he was right. I would've been more irritated by this had he told me half a story. "I believe you that you didn't know. I'm sorry that you found out the way you did."

He laughed sadly. "Yeah. Rex doesn't pull any punches."

"Nope, not the man you need to break news gently." I took him in my arms and squeezed him.

"Are we okay?" he asked quietly.

I hesitated, but then sighed. "Yeah. We have things we need to discuss obviously, but we have bigger issues to deal with right now, and I need you. Are you okay?" I pulled back and stroked his forehead. He was hot.

"I'll live," he muttered, but I wasn't convinced.

We both jumped a mile when the phone in my hand rang.

I drew back sharply, and we exchanged a fearful look, then I answered the call.

"Hello?" I barked into it.

"Put my baby-daddy on," Ella's stupid voice came down the phone as she laughed.

"Not a chance, cunt. You are talking to me, no one else. Mother to mother."

She hissed. "Do you have my daughter?"

"I want to know my daughter is fine and then I will do whatever you want."

I heard muffled whispering as I stalked out into the sitting room. I saw Rex and Lachlan hovering suspiciously over the baby and frowned at them. But then Ella came back on the line. "Tell Alex to check his phone," she clipped out.

"Check your phone," I barked at him as he was right behind me entering the sitting room.

He pulled it out and showed it to me. There was a picture taken of my little girl, fast asleep with today's newspaper next to her. I choked and it took me a few seconds to compose myself. "What do you want?" I asked her quietly.

"Oh, the price has gone up again," she chirped. "For the inconvenience of it all. I want six million dollars and my daughter, bitch, or you will *never* see your daughter again."

I stared at the baby in my apartment. She was nothing but a bargaining chip to drive the price up. This awful bitch didn't care about her. If she did, she wouldn't have said what she did about *me* seeing my daughter again. What about *her* seeing her daughter again?

"The price was half that originally, we only have that much now. You'll have to give us some time." I hated saying it. I wanted my daughter back right now, but we had to be smart about this. I saw Rex nodding his approval at my actions.

"8.00am tomorrow morning," she said. "I will text the details to you in a few. Alex drops it, alone, with *our* daughter and you can have yours back." She hung up and I felt sick to my stomach.

My shoulders drooped. I felt utterly helpless and defeated.

Lachlan was already on the phone with my grandfather. I knew he would put up the money without question, but I was hoping we wouldn't have to part with it. I was totally okay with Rex dealing with this *his* way.

I knew then that a tiny bit of my soul was lost to me. But I didn't care. I would lose my entire soul in a deal with the devil to save my daughter, my *family*. I was the same as Rex, and I was okay with that.

This grim thinking put me back on track. I stood up straighter and fixed Rex with a stare.

"I don't care how you have to find her; I don't care what you do to her when you do. Just. Find. Her."

He nodded his acceptance of my words, but then we all got a surprise as Alex spoke up.

"Wait," he said. "I think I have a plan."

16

~Alex~

I t was rash. A decision made on the spot when I saw how lost Cassie looked after the phone call.

"Just hear me out before you comment, okay?" I said as we gathered together in the middle of the room.

I cast a glance at my…daughter. She seemed to be happy enough, so I turned back to Cassie. I would have time later to really look at her. It was still sinking in.

"Okay," Cassie prompted when I stayed silent. "What is it?"

I took a deep breath. "I'm going to call her. Tell her I want to be with her and our daughter. She is that deluded; she will probably believe me…wait," I told Cassie as she opened her mouth to speak. "…hear me out. I can find where she is, take Scarlet and then you can follow me, and we'll take Ruby back."

I stopped speaking.

No one said anything.

Lachlan was the first to comment. "Are you insane?" he exclaimed. "Have your migraine drugs addled your brain?"

"No," I stated, a bit affronted by his incredulity at my

idea. Yes, my head was aching, and I felt sick and my eyesight was a bit blurry now and again, but I was thinking completely clearly.

"It's a good plan," Cassie said quietly. "It will work. She called you her "baby-daddy" on the phone."

"No!" Lachlan said. "We can't send him into the lion's den with no back up, especially feeling the way he is."

"I'm fine," I gritted out. "Rex?" He'd been quiet while he stared at me.

"It's our best option," he said quietly. "We can't be out there chasing our tails when we have a solid way in. We will be right behind you," he added forcefully.

I nodded. "I know. Sorry, Lach. Outvoted."

"Humph," he muttered and gave us all the finger.

"Get on board or get out of the way," Cassie snapped at him, but then shot him a soft smile to show she wasn't angry, just frustrated.

"On board," he sighed. "Obviously."

"But how will you call her? We don't have her number," Cassie said, chewing her lip.

I smiled at her and brandished my phone at her. "Yeah, we do. She was dumb enough to send me that pic from her phone while she was talking to you on the burner."

"Can't we just trace it, then?" she asked, fiddling with the phone in her hands, looking unsure.

"No time. This is the quickest way. If it doesn't work, we have other options." I took her by her hands. "Let me do this. We need Ruby back *tonight*."

I'd known it was the right thing to say. She nodded determinedly and all signs of uncertainty vanished. "Okay, yes. Okay. Please be careful."

"I will," I said to her and smiled.

I took back my hands and slipped off to the bedroom for a bit of privacy. I was going to have to say things to Ella that I didn't really want my wife overhearing, even if it was all a pack of lies.

I navigated to her number and connected the call.

Switched off.

I'd kind of expected that. So, I sent her a text message instead, saying we needed to talk about us and our daughter. I had no idea when she'd get it, or even if she would before 8.00am tomorrow, but I had to hope.

I went into the bathroom and took my glasses off. I splashed my face with cold water. I needed to get it together to pull this off. I leaned on the counter, the water dripping off my face when a message came through on my phone.

"No, already?" I whispered to myself as I picked it up and squinted at it as I replaced my glasses.

"Figured you would," the message said. "Call me."

I immediately hit redial and she answered on the second ring. "Hey, baby," she cooed.

I felt sick.

I pushed the nausea aside and smiled so that my tone sounded genuine. "Hey," I murmured back. "Our daughter is beautiful."

I heard a slight gasp before she said, "I know. She really is."

"I can't stop thinking about you, ever since Scarlet came here." I pulled a face at myself in the mirror and then turned around. I couldn't look at myself while I did this.

"And?" she asked, her voice hardening.

My next words had to be perfect or I would lose her. "I'm so excited to be a daddy," I said in a low tone. "I've wanted a child of my own for so long. You gave that to me. You have given me the perfect gift, Ella. I can't pretend that doesn't mean everything to me. Cassie…" I let out a weary sigh and squeezed my eyes shut as I told a lie. "She doesn't want any more kids. She's told us. I—I can't help thinking that I made a mistake being with her. I want a family, Ella. A *real* family. I want that with you and our daughter."

I held my breath as I waited.

"Really?" she croaked out.

I smiled again. "Yes, really."

"Oh, Alex," she breathed. "You have no idea how much I wanted to hear you say that. I love you. I love you so much."

I gripped the phone. "I love you too," I murmured, pretending I was saying it to Cassie. "Can I see you?" I risked it because that was what this whole damned façade was about.

She paused, but then said, "Yes. Bring Scarlet. I'm in room 402 of the Four Seasons."

I frowned down at the floor. The Four Seasons? No way Ella could afford that. I doubted very much that Teddy gave her any money to speak of so that he could keep her under this thumb. It all became clear to me in that moment that Ella was a puppet in someone else's scheme. Someone richer and more powerful. Someone who wanted to hurt Cassie just as much, but for different reasons entirely. This wasn't about *me* or jealousy of Cassie's life. This was about the money. They used the unforeseen Scarlet situation to their advantage to up the price. But who the hell was it?

"Alex?" Ella almost snapped at me.

"Yes, Room 402. I'll be there in half an hour to start our new life together."

"I can't wait!" she said excitedly again, and I relaxed. This had worked far better than I could have hoped for.

"See you soon," I murmured, and then hung up.

I raced out to the sitting room where I clearly interrupted a conversation that they didn't want me to be a part of.

"I've spoken to her," I said briskly, annoyed at them for excluding me. "Room 402 at the Four Seasons."

"What?" Rex said immediately catching what I was throwing at him. The other two were slower on the uptake.

"Yeah, there is definitely someone else involved in this. Someone bigger."

"Who?" Cassie demanded, but then gave me a grim look as she knew I didn't have the answer to that.

"Look, I've got to get going. I told Ella I'd be there in half an hour with Scarlet. Follow me and in exactly half an hour, wait outside the room for twenty minutes. I need to make sure that Ruby is in there. If we blow this a second time, it's game over. I'll…" I looked around hastily and found the perfect excuse. I went to the wine rack and pulled out a bottle of bubbly. "I'll leave the room to get ice if Ruby is in the room, that'll be your cue. Okay?" I shoved the bottle into Scarlet's diaper bag and put it over my shoulder.

"Wait," Rex said.

"No time," I interrupted him. "This is a solid plan. We do this exactly how I've laid it out. No deviations, no arguing about it. We go. Now." I scooped up Scarlet and grabbed the SUV keys. I stabbed the elevator button and climbed on board. "Now, people!" I yelled at them as they stood around looking like I'd lost my mind. As one, they moved forward and were in the elevator as the doors closed.

"You're a fucking lunatic," Lachlan muttered to me, but shoulder bumped me with a sexy smile. "I kinda like it."

I gave him a grin, fighting through the migraine that was quickly descending now.

As we got out of the elevator in the parking garage, Cassie grabbed my elbow and stood on her tiptoes to give me a soft kiss. "Do whatever you have to, okay?" She gave me a meaningful look and I gulped.

I nodded, hoping it wouldn't get that far. But Cassie clearly didn't put it past Ella to jump me the second I was in her clutches.

Rex grabbed the bag of weapons out of the SUV and chucked them into the Mustang.

"Where's the gun I gave you?" he asked me quietly.

"In the glove box." I indicated the Mustang with my chin and then strapped Scarlet into the car seat of the SUV. She was niggling and fussing. She was probably starving and needed changing and wanted her mother.

I leaned over to kiss her forehead. "You'll be with Mommy soon, sweet girl," I murmured to her and tucked a blanket round her to keep her warm. I popped a pacifier in her mouth that I found by rooting quickly through the bag and then I was in the driver's seat and gunning the engine.

"If Ruby isn't in the room, come home and wait for the drop. I'll get out as soon as I can." I nodded at Cassie, Rex and Lachlan and then I sped off towards the Four Seasons, hoping to fuck this was going to be as easy as it seemed to be playing out.

Somehow, though, I doubted it.

17

~Cassie~

I hunched further into the back seat, feeling cold. I wish that I'd had time to grab a jacket before we left again. Not that it would have helped, though. I was cold to the bone. This was the day from hell, and I wanted it over with and Ruby and Alex back home with me where they should be.

"Can't you go any faster?" I asked Rex.

"If we did that, we'd overtake Alex and then we'd be waiting at the hotel for him to arrive with our thumbs up our asses," Lachlan snapped at me, unusually punchy.

"What bit you on your ass?" I grumbled at him, just to say it. It was obvious that this day was getting to him too. How could it not?

He turned to me from the front seat. "Do you require an answer to that, my love?"

I lifted my chin at him and looked away. The dark night had started to rain, and it was flashing in the lights as we drove through the city.

"We shouldn't have sent Alex there the way he is,"

Lachlan exclaimed a moment later. "You know how bad those migraines get. He could get hurt, or worse."

"He'll be fine," I murmured, only to make myself feel better about it. I was also worried. Very worried. I had every conviction that she was going to jump on him the moment he stepped through the door...and he would have to play along. It made my stomach clench even more thinking about them in a steamy lip lock.

"I hope you're right," Lachlan muttered.

We descended into silence again until Rex said, "We're here."

I looked up and saw the Four Seasons lit up against the dark sky. We'd parked across the road and further down, while Alex had pulled up right outside. He was getting Scarlet out of the SUV as a waiting valet hovered close by. He looked steady, but his movements were slower than they normally would be.

"Let's go," I said, ready to climb out.

"Wait," Rex said, holding up his hand. "We've got ten minutes yet before the twenty-minute countdown. We'll let him get inside before we follow. We know where we're going."

I waited impatiently, staring at the hotel. It was swanky. I adored it there, but it was definitely way out of Ella's price range. Who could possibly be the money behind this kidnapping? Also, if they had money why did they want more?

As we watched Alex walk inside with his daughter in his arms, I sighed, coming to the realization that the child wasn't going anywhere.

"We're going to have to take her in, aren't we?" I asked quietly.

Lachlan turned to me, his stinky attitude disappearing as he looked at me briefly before he caught Rex's eye. They exchanged a look but then Rex focused back on the hotel as Lachlan turned back to me.

"What?" I asked. "What do you know?"

Rex pulled something out of his inside jacket pocket, his eyes still trained on the hotel. He waggled it at me and then shoved it away again.

"What's that?" I asked, although I had a fairly good idea.

"A DNA swab," Lachlan said.

"You don't believe that she's Alex's child?" I ventured carefully.

"We think it would be stupid of us to believe anything that woman says or does. So what, that the hospital confirmed Alex as the father. She could've given them anyone's DNA to compare it to saying it was Alex's. We need to be one hundred percent sure from our end. That's all."

I started to smile, but Lachlan's next words stopped me, and I bit the inside of my cheek instead.

"You know he will be devastated if she isn't his. He's made it very clear he wants a child. He's older than us, he's thinking differently to us. We think we have all the time in the world. He is a few years in front of us, he wants a child. Soon."

"I know," I whispered, feeling awful for wishing that Scarlet wasn't his. I *did* know how much he wanted a child. He had been very vocal about his desire. I was planning on giving it to him when Ruby was a little bit older. Yeah, Rex and Lachlan would suffer, but hopefully it wouldn't take that long for us to conceive and then he would be happy. It was a very real, yet secret fear of mine that he would want to leave me if we never had our own child. I'd be happy with just Ruby, but I was fully aware of how much it meant to him.

Rex snuck out of the car and opened the trunk. I knew he was getting the guns back out. This time, I was going to make him give me one.

He slid back in with the bag and chucked it at Lachlan again, who grunted his protest.

"Here," Rex said to me, handing me one of his black hoodies that he wore to the gym.

I took it gingerly and gave it a delicate sniff. It was freshly laundered, so I smiled my thanks and put it on. It was miles too big for me, but at least I wasn't cold anymore. Plus, it would cover up my weapon.

I gave Rex a grim look. "I want a gun this time. Alex had one last time, so give me one to replace his."

He sighed and handed me a small handgun that fit in my hand perfectly. It was heavy in spite of its size. "Do you even have any idea how to use it?" he asked.

"No," I said sullenly. "But how hard can it be? Point and shoot."

"Uhm," Lachlan started, but Rex shushed him and proceeded to give me a ten second run through. I was lost so I was going with *my* way. Point it and if I have to, fire the damn thing.

"Got it?" he growled.

I nodded and shoved it in the back of my jeans like he did with his.

He gave me a worried look, but then said, "Time to go."

We all got out and crossed the road.

"Wait," Lachlan said. "Through the front door?"

"We have no choice," Rex said. "We haven't had time, nor do we have time to do recon. We have no idea where the back is, how to get to the service entrance or what we might find once we do. This is the only option." He paused to give me a scathing once over. "Try to look like you belong," he murmured.

"Hey!" I snapped at him. "I *do* belong. Bellingham billionaire, remember?"

"It's hard to forget," he muttered back.

"What's *that* supposed to mean?" I raised my voice and then slammed my lips shut. We were supposed to be flying under the radar. Although I *did* stick out like a sore thumb in this hoodie.

He blew out a breath and looked away.

"Say it," I gritted out, grabbing his arm.

"If you weren't, we wouldn't be here. They've targeted you because you *are* a Bellingham billionaire."

I hissed as his words cut across me.

"That's not fair," Lachlan murmured. "But shelve this. We have to get going. Alex has risked a lot for us to rescue Ruby. Now move."

He stalked off and Rex and I exchanged mutinous glares. I threw my shoulders back and sashayed forward, slipping my hand into Lachlan's so that I wasn't ambling along by myself. Rex slunk behind us and soon we were in the elevator, holding our breath as it dinged on the fourth floor and we stepped out.

Now, we had to wait and hope that Alex showed up at the ice machine.

18

~Rex~

I hated this. I was used to being organized and meticulous in my planning. I now had Lachlan and Cassie with me, who really had no clue what to do, along with my daughter in a dangerous situation. I had to be focused and cold, but how could I do that when she was in the room and could get hurt. I had to be both cold and conscious of the consequences. Something that had never been an issue before.

Cassie was at the front of our group huddled in the supply closet that I'd seen and had a view of the room door and the ice machine a little further down the hall. She was fidgeting and it was putting me on edge. I knew that I'd been unduly harsh with her before, but I couldn't help thinking that I was right. This had everything to do with her being who she was. It was always going to be that way. I saw only one way out and she wouldn't like it. I would never ask her to give up her legacy but living in the penthouse was not an option anymore. We were going to have to move onto a secure estate out in the suburbs. Cassie loved the city, the vibrancy, the buzz, but it just wasn't safe anymore. We had been forced into accepting a new normalcy and that meant security around the clock on an impenetrable estate.

I wasn't looking forward to it. I'd hoped it would never happen. I wasn't cut out for sprawling properties. I liked closed in and compact. Call me weird, but I found comfort in the near claustrophobia of five of us living in close quarters. It had also become apparent in the last few hours that I could no longer be away from Ruby for even a second. I would have to quit my job to be around to watch over them all of the time. I was sure I could handle being a stay-at-home dad. I would enjoy it.

The thought of it *gave* me joy. It was something that had been sorely lacking from my life until Cassie and I fell in love.

"Stop it," I murmured to her as she stood on my toe, she was bouncing around that much. "You need to relax or you're going to blow this rescue."

I gave it to her straight and she froze. I heard her labored breathing, but she had listened to me and was trying.

I loved her so much in that moment.

I leaned over to kiss the top of her head. "Sorry for what I said. I don't blame you," I murmured.

Lachlan took my hand and squeezed it briefly before letting me go again. He knew how hard it was for me to say that out loud. Sorry, just didn't come naturally to me. I was resolute in my convictions. I had fuck all to apologize for. Except when it came to my wife. I seemed to disappoint her frequently.

"It's okay," she whispered back, leaning back into me slightly, but never taking her eyes off the crack in the door that gave us an extremely limited view. "We are all fraught."

I kissed her again on top of her head. She was the sweetest thing. An angel. She always forgave me. I used to think that one day I would do something that would ruin her faith in me, but I hadn't. Not even being an ex-contract killer had turned her from me. I was the luckiest man alive to have her in my life. I knew that many women wouldn't be so understanding, and I wondered how she'd found it in her to move on from it so quickly. Maybe she wasn't so different to me. She was fierce and would do anything for her family. I knew the second that I handed her that gun in the car that she wouldn't hesitate to use it if she needed to. I hoped she didn't have to. For her sake and for our daughter's. It wasn't something that I wanted her to live with. But I also knew that if I'd tried to keep her away, she wouldn't have and would have potentially ruined our last chance to get our daughter back and find out who the hell was pulling the strings here, because it sure as shit wasn't Ella.

"How much longer?" Cassie asked.

I checked my watch. "A few minutes." Alex was cutting it fine. I knew he had to extricate himself from the situation without suspicion and that was going to take him time. He wasn't rolling at a hundred percent. It was against my better judgment to let him come here, but he was also our best hope. It was a sound plan, as long as Ruby was in there.

We all hitched our breath as the door to the room opened and we saw Alex. I pulled the door even closer shut so that we could barely see him, but he was walking to the ice machine.

"Ruby," Cassie breathed and took a step forward.

I pulled her back by the hood on the sweatshirt. "Not so fast," I murmured. "I go first."

She started to protest but shut it pretty quickly when she realized that I was right.

"Follow me in, but do not move from behind me. We know Ruby is in there, but we don't know where, okay? We need to ascertain her whereabouts *before* we get her back."

She nodded and so did Lachlan. "Weapons out?" she asked, reaching around the back.

I smiled at her. She was so eager to get the gun in her hand. It was so fucking sexy, I wanted to take her right there. "Yes, weapons out," I said and then pushed around her to poke my head out of the door. We were so conspicuous, it clawed at me. This wasn't happening with my usual finesse but getting to my daughter the quickest way possible was all that mattered.

I didn't see anyone in the hallway, so I pushed the door out further and gripped the handles of the two handguns at my back.

"Ready?" I murmured.

"Yes," they both whispered back and then my focus went sharp. I blocked out everything else as I strode to the door and kicked it in, this time knowing that my daughter was behind it. It gave me all the confidence I needed to draw my two weapons and level them at either side of the room as I took in Ella, two goons, the two babies next to each other on the far side and...

"What the fucking hell?" Cassie shrieked right behind me in my ear.

Alex came storming back through the door, wielding the ice bucket like a weapon and then all hell broke loose.

19

~Cassie~

The shit had totally hit the fan since we entered the room, but all I could focus on was getting to my daughter. Once I had her in my arms, I could figure out what the hell Derek was doing here.

He and Rex were currently grappling with each other, having thankfully stowed the weapons to go at it fists flying.

Lachlan was battling with the other two men, that looked so shady it made me shudder. Alex had Ella with her arm behind her back and was pushing her to her knees as she shrieked obscenities at him, at me and everyone in the room. He was squinting fiercely as the pain of his migraine was getting too much for him, but he was on his feet and wrestling Ella into submission. I scooped up Ruby and cooed at her, jiggling her. She was half asleep, but with all the noise and commotion she'd woken and had started to scream. I cast a glance at Scarlet, her name only just registering with me and I scowled back at Ella.

"Fucking psycho," I muttered and bent down to coo at the baby to keep her calm, although in all fairness, she was pretty chilled out. Maybe she was used to this kind of activity. That broke my heart. My Uncle Teddy, to me anyway, was a gentleman, but I was getting all sorts of lessons in how wrong that perception was. He was a stranger that I barely recognized. Who knows how he treated Ella and her child? Alex's child.

As I jiggled Ruby, I watched as Alex subdued Ella, who was still fighting like a hellcat, by tying his belt around her wrists as he knelt on her back. He slumped as soon as her hands were bound and I went to him, helping him up and then shoving him into a corner to sit down.

"Are you able?" I asked him.

"Yeah," he replied as I knew he would.

I thrust Ruby at him, regardless, knowing he would protect her with his life, even if he wanted to throw up and curl up into a ball while doing it.

I pulled the gun back out of my jeans and spun around, aiming it at someone. The other men were all still in a fist fight, bodies and furniture flying everywhere. Luckily, *my* men were on top. They were both enormous men, trained to fight and even though Lachlan was more a lover than a fighter, he was fighting for his family. He smashed a fist into the face of one, and a booted foot to the other and then I heard a muffled *ping*.

Gaping, I looked at Rex and he stood up, gun in hand, wiping the sweat from his brow as he glared down at Derek who was dead on the floor.

"Fuck," I muttered and then got knocked off my feet as my concentration was broken. Ella had struggled to her feet and had kicked mine out from under me.

"You bitch!" she shrieked and lifted her foot to kick me.

There was only one thing for me to do and that was point my gun at her.

She froze, but her evil smile stayed in place. "Your mother was right about you," she hissed. "You are a filthy slut and you don't deserve the life you've been handed." She kicked me in the ribs, and I let out a breath as the wind went out of me. I groaned and tried to focus on what she'd said.

"My mother?" I muttered in confusion. "When did you…"

"What in the blazes…?"

We all turned at the startled exclamation and saw none other than Suzanne standing with the door open, her hand wrapped around the edge.

The lock was busted from when Rex kicked it in, but Alex tearing through after us, had slammed it shut behind him.

"Mother?" I croaked out. "What is going on?" I struggled to my feet and on instinct pointed the gun at her.

She was staring down at Derek, her face an impenetrable mask. "I should've known teaming up with *you* was going to end like this," she sneered at Ella after a beat.

"What?" I yelled at her. "This was all *you*? Why?"

She turned that cruel sneer on me. It hardened my heart and I stumbled closer to her; the gun still leveled at her. "*Why?*" I demanded coldly.

Out of the corner of my eye I saw Rex grab Ella firmly by the arm and haul her off to the side, away from me.

Lachlan had knocked out the other two men, so he edged closer to me, slowly, his hands raised. He thought I was a loose cannon, but he couldn't have been more wrong.

I was totally focused, totally calm. I had my finger on the trigger.

I belatedly wondered if I'd taken the safety off.

It didn't matter. My mother was taking me seriously all of a sudden.

"Why?" I gritted out.

"Why do you think?" she snarled at me. "You are going to take everything from me. I had to do something. It's not like you were going to share the wealth after all." Her scoff just incensed me further.

"Are you serious?" I snapped at her. "You kidnapped my daughter! You put me through hell! You teamed up with that stupid bitch, that you *know* has a problem with me, and for what? Money, so that you didn't lose your precious lifestyle."

"He was cutting me out!" she shrieked at me, completely losing control of her temper. She was growling like a rabid dog. "My own fucking father was just going to toss me aside, for *you*! I wanted to make you pay, I wanted to hurt you!" She stuck her hand in her purse and pulled out a gun that she pointed at me. We were in a standoff.

My stomach lurched. She truly hated me. She never wanted me or cared about me at all. All she saw when she looked at me was the *thing* that was taking her money from her. It made me sick, it made me sad, but it also made me angry.

She'd stolen my daughter and used her to get to me.

"If you had a problem with me, you should've left my daughter out of it," I said to her coolly, lowering the gun.

She looked at it and smirked. "I knew you didn't have the balls," she said, keeping her gun in my face.

"Maybe not," I replied. "But *he* does." I turned my back on her knowing that Rex was behind me, his gun pointed at my mother.

There is no way on this green earth that he would allow *anyone*, not even my own mother, to threaten me at gunpoint.

I stashed the gun in the back of my jeans and took Ruby from Alex as Lachlan helped him to his feet.

My hands were steady as I walked past Rex with the other men behind me.

"Do what you have to do to keep our family safe," I told him coldly.

"You little bitch!" she shrieked, her gun still trained on me as I walked past. "You want me gone from your life, little girl, you will fucking do it yourself. Coward! I knew I'd raised a complete loser!" Her eyes were wild as I stopped and turned to face her. She had completely lost control. Her hand was shaking so badly.

"A year ago, that would have devastated me," I said to her

quietly. "Now, I don't give a flying fuck what you think of me. You are dead to me whether you are actually dead or not. I'll leave that to my husband to decide. Do bear in mind that you took his daughter, and now you're pointing a gun at her."

I watched as she froze. Rex had the gun pointed at her head from millimeters away.

"Shoot her!" Ella screamed and I only noticed her still clutched in Rex's hand tightly. I'd been completely focused on my mother.

It was unclear which one of us she was talking about. Probably both of us. More likely me.

"Shoot that fucking bitch!" she yelled.

"I'm done here," I informed them loftily and once again turned my back, leaving Rex to do whatever he wanted to do.

I got to the door. I reached for the handle, then froze.

"Don't move or your husband gets it," a man growled at me.

I turned around slowly to see one of the men that Lachlan had put down, unsteadily on his feet, a gun pointed at Rex.

He was cornered with Ella clutched in his fist.

"I want my cut," he growled.

"We don't have the money," I said.

"I want my money," he repeated slowly as if I was stupid.

"I said, we don't have it," I gritted out and then thrust Ruby at Lachlan, who dropped Alex and clutched her as I pulled my gun back out and pointed it at the man.

He gave me a cursory glance but didn't look worried. "Then, he dies."

He pulled the trigger.

The silencer on the end made it sound like a *ping*, which I only registered after I acted on instinct.

"Rex!" I shouted and pulled the trigger myself.

The shot went off, recoiling and making me stumble as I hadn't been ready for it at all.

Another shot and a *ping-ping* and then Rex was hauling

me out of the room, picking me up and slinging me over his shoulder fireman style, as the world slowed down and went completely silent save for the words from my husband.

"We need to get out of here. Now."

20

~Lachlan~

I moved.

I didn't hesitate for even a second when Rex yelled at us to get going. We had created a shitstorm that would have the cops raining merry hell down on us if they even found a trace of us in this room.

"Wait," Alex muttered, his hand on his forehead. "Scarlet."

"Dammit," I grit out and shoved Alex forward out of the room. "I'll get her."

I watched him stumble after Rex and Cassie and then spun to lunge forward to pick up the second baby. I jiggled them both and scooped up the two diaper bags as well. I looked across the carnage we'd caused and walked quickly out of the room, attempting to pull the door closed with my foot.

"The other guy," I hissed at Rex.

"I know," he snarled and dumped Cassie into the elevator, shoved me and the babies inside, and then not so gently guided poor Alex in as well. He reached in and pushed the button for three floors up. I frowned at him.

"Get out, go down one flight of stairs and get back on, preferably with the other elevator," he instructed.

I nodded and didn't ask twice. He was the boss in this situation. I hadn't got a fucking clue. I was rolling with it, babies in arms.

Cassie took Ruby from me, silent but steady.

No one said a word as Rex stood back and the doors shut.

I didn't like to think what he was going to do once he got back to the room. Probably no one did and that's why, out of taciturn agreement, we didn't say anything.

We got out, three floors up and headed for the stairwell. We went down a flight and then waited for the first elevator to head on up and then we waited for the second elevator to pick us up again.

Once we got back to the SUV, Alex handed me the key and got in. I strapped Scarlet in the baby seat, as Cassie slid in with Ruby on her lap. It wasn't ideal, but it was all we had. I climbed in and drove off. Rex wouldn't want us hanging around and he had to get the Mustang back to the penthouse.

The drive home was quiet and felt way longer than it should've. My phone rang twice, Eliza, but I ignored it. I caught Cassie grimacing at me in the rearview mirror and her face stayed that way until we finally pulled into the parking garage and she got out with Ruby.

She marched off, leaving us to follow.

"You okay?" I asked Alex, breaking the uneasy silence.

"Yeah," he croaked. "You?"

"Yeah," I croaked back.

That was all we had to say to each other.

❧❧❧

ONCE WE GOT BACK UPSTAIRS, I put the sleeping Scarlet into Ruby's crib in her room, knowing that Ruby wouldn't be out of Cassie's sight for even a second and wouldn't be using it. Then I helped Alex into bed.

He groaned in relief and fell promptly asleep.

I smiled at him and removed his glasses and his shoes and tucked him up.

Then I headed back to Cassie to see her cuddled up with Ruby on the sofa.

"You okay?" I asked her. This was about my limit with vocabulary at that point.

"Yeah. You?"

"Yeah."

I rolled my eyes at the repetitive repertoire and turned to get us both a stiff drink.

She accepted hers with a grateful smile and then we jumped out of our skins when the elevator dinged, and Rex strode out.

"Err," I muttered, looking at my watch.

He growled at me. "I'm not hauling five bodies away from a crowded, well-lit, secure hotel all by myself. The cops will have to find them. Especially as one of them is Cassie's mom. A Bellingham," he added quietly.

"You did the right thing," she said coldly. "She pulled the trigger to save her own skin."

"I took care of the last guy and swept the room clean. There's nothing for it now but to wait." His look said it all. He had major doubts that we would come out of this untarnished.

"We protect Cassie," I stated loud and clear.

She looked at me with a frown and started to shake her head.

"You are our wife. You are Ruby's mother. She needs you. We protect you plain and simple."

"Agreed," Rex said just as firmly.

"Did I…? Did he…?" She bit her lip.

Rex took her hand and squeezed it. "No," he said, but I knew it was a lie.

Cassie had shot the asshole that had fired at Rex in the neck. He would have bled out before we left the room.

"You injured him enough for us to get away. I finished him off," Rex said stiffly.

She stifled her sob and nodded. I could see the relief on her face and see her shoulders drop slightly from the tension that she'd been carrying.

"I'm sorry," she wept, drawing him to her. "I'm sorry that you had to do that."

"Hey," he said, taking her hands again. "I would do it all again and more for you and our daughter. Our family," he said, cutting his gaze to me quickly.

I nodded and he looked away.

He knew I was aware of his lie. I would take it to my grave to save Cassie the burden of carrying it. Rex would suffer, that adding to his guilt, but I would help him deal with it.

"What do we do next?" she asked.

"Nothing. Absolutely nothing. We wait for the cops to show up and that's it."

"Grandaddy and Grandma knew Ruby was kidnapped. What the hell do we say about that?" she asked. She was completely calm. She was thinking clearly and rationally and had brought up the only thought that was swimming around my head as well.

There was no way we were getting out of this with our hands clean.

"I already called William," Rex said. "I told him that I tracked down Ella and got Ruby back three hours ago. I apologized for the delay, but we were thrilled to get our daughter back and lost track of time. He accepted it and said he and Ruby will be by tomorrow first thing."

"But…" Cassie started to interrupt him.

He held his hand up. "As far as we knew Suzanne and Derek were conducting their own search and that's all we know," he added firmly.

"And what about Scarlet?" I added gently.

"We took her from Teddy's this afternoon," he replied

with a shrug. He reached into the pockets of his leather jacket and dumped a pile of burner phones on the table. "We do need to get rid of these."

I gathered them up and went to the kitchen. I shoved them in the microwave and pushed start. We all watched as they lit up, frazzled and died, killing the microwave with it.

I then scooped them into individual sandwich bags and tied them off. "I'll see these into the Hudson."

Rex nodded at me as I bent to kiss Cassie and Ruby good-bye. "Be right back," I said and left, pulling my phone out of my back pocket to call Eliza back.

"What's up?" I asked her as I descended in the elevator.

"Nothing, sugar. Just checking in," she replied.

"You okay?" I asked and cringed.

"Yeah. You?" she asked back.

I thumped my fist on the elevator mirror with a shake of my head. "Perfect," I muttered and hung up after saying goodbye.

I made my way out into the late night.

I walked until I came to the river and then one by one, threw the damaged burner phones into it. It wasn't perfect, but it was good enough.

That was all we could hope for now.

Life was never going to be perfect again. There was just far too much baggage weighing us down. I hoped that it didn't affect us, but that was unrealistic.

I sighed and headed back to the penthouse, trying to shake off the feeling of dread that was enveloping me. I had to be my usual optimistic self around Cassie and Ruby. She looked to me to be the one to bring a bit of light into Rex's darkness. I felt he was going to need it now more than ever.

21

~Cassie~

A week had passed, and I still didn't know how one or all of us hadn't been arrested for that night which I couldn't get out of my head.

I was sitting in the front pew of the family's church, cold, frozen almost, with Ruby on my lap. She was wiggling about, fussing so Lachlan took her from me. Alex was on my other side, but he had Scarlet with him.

I didn't know how we'd gotten here. We'd barely spoken, the four of us, in over three days.

I kept replaying the incident in my head.

The man shot at Rex but hit Ella instead.

I fired my gun and Rex said I grazed him but didn't kill him.

He fell.

The recoil from the gun had made me stumble so my mother, who'd fired her gun at me, missed and then Rex had killed her.

Head shot.

Instant death.

My hands started to shake as I stared at the coffin at the

front of the church. I could tell no one except my husbands how I was feeling about this, and even then, I was struggling to deal with it.

My mother had tried to kill me.

If I hadn't stumbled, she probably would have hit me.

I blinked as I heard my Grandma sobbing her heart out.

I looked up at Grandaddy. He was giving his daughter's eulogy, but I hadn't heard a word.

My father was a no-show, not surprisingly, and there was no way I could get up there and speak about her.

I waited until he'd finished, and he gave me a sad smile as he made his way back to his seat.

"The babies shouldn't be here," I blurted out.

I'd wanted Ruby with me, I never wanted her out of my sight again, but it was wrong to bring her here. Both of them.

"I'll take them home," Alex said gently.

I nodded and watched as Lachlan handed Ruby over. He slipped out, juggling the two babies and I realized that I didn't want to be here either. It was hypocritical, and I was so sure I was going to send us all down by acting suspiciously or saying the wrong thing.

"Take me home," I muttered to Lachlan.

He stood up straight away and Rex followed.

I blindly followed them, ignoring my grandfather calling out to me. I would call him later, explain that it was too much.

We caught up with Alex outside in the bright sun. It warmed my skin, covered in a black silk dress that made my skin feel like it wanted to crawl off my body. I wanted to rip it off and burn it.

"Wait, I don't want to go home. Not yet," I said. "Let's drop the babies with Aurora and then go to the club. I need… I need…" I choked and Lachlan wrapped his arms around me. I sank against him and let out a sob, but then pulled myself together. I didn't want to cry in front of my daughter. I pushed away from Lachlan.

"I just need to forget," I stated and walked to the car.

I waited for them to catch up and then we were on our way back to the penthouse and Aurora.

I left the babies there with her, under strict instruction not to move from the apartment no matter what and to not let anyone in. The two security guards outside the front door did nothing to ease my anxiety.

As I slipped back into the car, I felt the guilt overwhelm me and I silently wept, staring out of the window as we drove the short way to *Corsets & Collars*.

❦

Ten minutes later, Rex pulled up and turned to face me and Alex in the back seat. He sighed and pulled an envelope out of his inside jacket pocket.

"I know what Ella said, but...we had to be sure, yeah, so don't get pissed off." He handed the envelope to Alex, who looked at it in confusion that turned to anger.

"He said don't get pissed off," Lachlan said. "Just read it."

"Have you?" Alex asked, turning it over in his hands.

"No, of course not," Lachlan said, but in spite of having an excellent poker face, I knew he was lying. I'd known him for too many years not to know his face as well as my own.

I bit my lip and stared at the envelope. Such a big part of me hoped that she wasn't his, but that just added to the great big pile of stinking guilt that had settled on me since the... incident. I gulped. I couldn't bring myself to say quintuple homicide.

Again, I couldn't believe that we hadn't been implicated. We'd been suspected, I was convinced, but none of us had been arrested yet. I said, yet, as I fully believed that we would be. It was about to give me a nervous breakdown and I started to fidget.

Alex took that as a sign to open the envelope.

I waited with bated breath and then felt like a piece of

utter garbage when his face fell, and he folded the letter up and pocketed it.

"Not mine," he stated, staring out of the car window.

"I'm sorry," I murmured to him, taking his hand.

"Wait," Rex said as Alex was about to pull away from me and get out of the car. "There's more." He handed *me* an envelope and I stared at it.

"Well, she isn't *mine*," I commented.

"Just open it," Rex gritted out.

I tore the envelope and unfolded the letter. I read and my eyes went wide, but I realized that I wasn't that surprised.

"Uncle Teddy's," I stated. "So, she's my cousin."

Rex nodded.

Lachlan gave me a serious look that portrayed what he felt about this situation.

"We'll talk about this later. Please can we go inside and forget now?" I asked anxiously.

"Yes," Alex said firmly and took me by the hand as he exited the car, pulling me out with him.

I felt a frisson of nerves shoot through me. He had gone into alpha mode and while that thrilled me, it also made me a little bit nervous. I had no idea what to expect from him. He hadn't really delved into the role yet; he'd only dipped his toe and who knew what he would do in a room full of debauchery.

But despite that, I couldn't wait to find out.

I hurried behind him as he strode quickly into the club, with Lachlan and Rex close behind us.

Alex paused and let Lachlan lead us to a private room next to his office. This was ours. We no longer felt it appropriate to have the playroom at the penthouse, so Lachlan had arranged for one here, solely for our use. All of our toys were here now, except for one or two essential, spur of the moment, instruments at home. It was locked up tight, Lachlan having one key and I had the other. It had a plush black carpet, black silk walls, fake candles flickering around the room, giving it a seductive, yet somehow also an eerie glow.

"Are you okay?" Alex murmured, a look of concern on his handsome face.

"Yes," I said, and pulled away, finally stripping off the black dress and my underwear. I kicked off my shoes, my feet sinking into the soft carpet and knelt before Lachlan, my head bowed.

"Punish me, Daddy, please. I've been so naughty," I muttered.

His hand went into my hair and he gripped a fistful tightly, lifting my head up.

"Have you now?" he asked, giving me a penetrating look. "Tell Daddy what you've done."

I whimpered. I wasn't into confession. I didn't want to bare my soul.

He let me go and walked away from me. He opened a drawer and then came back to wind my hair up into a tight bun on top of my head, shoving pins into it to keep it secure. Then he handed Alex a pair of nipple clamps.

I couldn't resist looking up to see his reaction. I wanted to giggle but then I remembered why we were here, and I lowered my eyes again.

"Here," Rex murmured to him, taking them off him and kneeling in front of me. "Like this."

I gasped as he attached one and left the other to Alex.

Then Rex left me and stripped naked. Lachlan followed him.

Alex stood up and looked down at me. "Stand up," he ordered me.

I did.

He grabbed my hands and attached a pair of cuffs to my wrists. Then he led me over to a chain hanging down that was attached to the ceiling. He reached for it and hooked them to it.

"Kneel," he instructed softly.

I did and it forced my arms up above my head. My shoulders groaned in protest, but I didn't utter a sound.

He stripped off his jacket and threw it in the corner.

His shirt followed and then his shoes, socks and pants. He was going commando, which made me go damp. I loved knowing he was walking around unencumbered. They all did it now and again and I found it a massive turn on to wonder every day what they were wearing.

He walked over to the far side of the dimly lit room. I heard him opening drawers and then he stopped suddenly.

He walked back to me and I saw that he had a riding crop in his hand.

I shivered as he slapped it against his palm.

"How naughty?" he asked.

"Very."

"Do you want me to punish you before your Daddy does?"

My breath quickened at those words. "Yes."

"Yes, what?" he barked at me.

"Yes, please, *Master*."

The silence was deafening.

Rex went to Alex. "She has defined your role for you," he whispered, pushing him forward slightly. "Tell her you accept it…or not."

I waited, holding my breath. My arms started to ache with the tension of being suspended above my head.

"Is that what you really want from me?" he asked me, crouching down and lifting my chin with the riding crop. "You want it from *me*, not *him*?"

I glanced quickly at Rex. I knew he would never take this role with me again and in that moment, I realized I didn't want him to. I looked firmly back at Alex. "Yes," I stated.

"Then your Master, I shall be," he said, dropping the riding crop to my pussy and gently rubbing the tip of the handle over my clit. "You will do whatever I tell you to in this room."

I nodded. "Yes, Master."

He increased the pressure on the riding crop, circling it slowly, enticingly. "Does that feel good?"

"Yes," I moaned.

"You aren't allowed to come," he instructed me.

I knew he was going to say that, knew he'd want that power over me, but it still stung. I was ready, really ready to lose myself in an orgasm that rocked my body and rattled the chains holding me in place.

"Yes, Master."

He removed the crop and leaned in close to me. "What do you want, Cassie? What do you want that will turn you on?"

I brought my eyes level with his and gave him a soft smile. "You know what I want to see."

He smirked at me and stood up.

I watched as he went over to Lachlan and, with a hand on the back of his neck, kissed him. It was a passionate kiss that made me wet and pant with longing. I wanted to be part of it.

Lachlan wrapped his hand around Alex's cock and started to tug him gently.

I groaned as I watched it.

Lachlan pulled away and said to me. "Daddy wants Rex to lick your pussy while you watch him jerk off your Master. Rise up."

I did as I was told. But as submissive as I was right now to Lachlan and Alex, Rex was *my* Sub and he needed to hear it from me.

"Come here and lick my pussy," I ordered him.

He crawled over to me, eager to do as I asked.

I rose up higher on my knees and parted my legs so that Rex could get to my clit and flick it with that amazing tongue. He flipped over and laid on his back, his face under my pussy.

"Oh, yes," I moaned and fell completely into the roles.

Master barked, "No coming!" and I groaned with frustration.

"Quiet, little girl," Daddy said. "You will be happy to obey your Master."

I nodded quickly and then was forced to watch my Daddy go down on my Master and take his cock in his mouth.

"Fuck, yes," Master muttered, his eyes on me.

My Sub continued to tongue fuck me to the point where I was about to cry with holding onto my climax.

"Please," I begged as I felt that sought-after rush in my veins.

"No!" Master said.

He looked down at Daddy sucking his cock for all he was worth, and I felt the tears seep out of my eyes. I wanted to touch, to feel, to kiss, to come and I had none of it. I was bound, forced to only watch the most erotic experience and it was as I'd asked.

I was being punished for my sins. The guilt that was eating me alive had an outlet and I let it wash over me as I stifled my choke of arousal when my Master came in Daddy's mouth, pumping his hips as he gently fucked Daddy's mouth through his climax.

I closed my eyes. "Eyes open!" Daddy ordered me.

I opened them again. "Please, let me come, Daddy, please."

He crawled over to me, leaving my Master panting after his release. He scooted around Rex and came to kiss me, sweeping his tongue coated with my Master's cum over mine. He gripped my throat and pulled away.

"No, Princess. It isn't time yet. I promise you when I allow it, you will feel every nerve ending set on fire as it tears through your gorgeous body, hardening those aching buds even more, wetting your pretty pussy until you are dripping, making your clit thud until you can't take it anymore."

"Fuck," I moaned softly and felt my clit twitch and then it was happening. I couldn't help it.

I cried out as Rex fucked me with his tongue, groaning as I flooded his mouth with my juices.

"Oh, naughty, naughty, Princess," Daddy muttered, shaking his head at me.

"I'm sorry," I cried. "Punish me, Daddy, please, punish me."

"All in good time," he said and sat back.

"Tell your Sub to stop," Master said to me from across the room. "You are a bad girl and you don't get to have your clit licked anymore."

"Stop," I croaked to my Sub. "Stop."

He did as he was ordered and moved away from me.

I then let out a cry of another kind, the tears still dropping onto my cheeks as my Master took my Sub and helped him to his feet.

"I want to know what it feels like to kiss you," Master murmured to my Sub and I wept harder.

They were about to do everything I wanted them to and all I could do was watch as they did it.

I slumped back down to the carpet, my arms going higher above my head again.

It was torture.

But there was no doubt in my mind that I deserved it and more.

22

~Alex~

Rex's dark eyes bored into mine. I suddenly felt a pang of nerves as he was waiting for me to make the first move. I'd started it and he expected me to finish it.

I leaned forward, trying to ignore Cassie's tears. It was difficult. She was in pain, the guilt overwhelming her after what had happened the other night. We all wanted to forget, *needed* to forget, but it wasn't going to happen.

I pushed aside my wife's pain, along with my own at discovering that Scarlet wasn't mine. It wasn't like I hadn't thought about it constantly in the last few days. But I'd really thought – hoped – that she was mine. I knew that hurt Cassie as well.

I pressed my lips against Rex's knowing that it would take away some of Cassie's pain, at the same time it would cause it. She wanted this for us. She wanted us all together. But she wanted to be a part of it. So she should, as well.

Rex took pity on me and opened up. He pushed his tongue into my mouth, and I couldn't help the moan that escaped me. The kiss was soft, a complete contrast to how I expected it to be.

"Did you like that?" he asked me, as he pulled away.

"Yes," I breathed.

"Do you want me to do it again?"

"Yes."

He leaned in and my hand automatically went to his cock. It was erect and huge. My hand circled around him and I tugged gently.

He moaned into my mouth and drew back slightly.

Cassie's sobs stopped and that made me feel better about continuing.

"I'm wondering something," Rex said to me, giving me a heated look that made my own cock bounce in response.

"What's that?" I asked, puzzled.

"I like showing you how things work in this world," he whispered to me. "I wonder if you like it too."

"I do," I replied and licked my lips, not having a clue where he was going with this.

"I don't want to be your Master or your Daddy," he said quietly as Lachlan came closer with a curious look on his face. "But I want to teach you, show you…"

"Yes," I interrupted him.

"I want to be your mentor," he continued, ignoring me.

"Ooh," Cassie moaned, her chains rattling as she struggled to get to her feet. "Please let me out of here."

"Not yet," Lachlan said. "Sit down, Princess."

"Please," she begged.

I was about to let her off the hook when Rex grabbed my arm.

"No," he said. "Do not go to her." He reached for my cock and jerked me off roughly to draw my attention back to his own cock that was still in my hand.

"She's fine," Rex said, and I looked to Lachlan to confirm.

He nodded.

I didn't look at her again.

I heard her sit down, the chains clattering in an otherwise silent room.

"Wait," I said to Rex.

I walked over to the drawers and pulled one open. I remember from earlier that this one was full of dildos. I reached for a huge black one with a suction cup on the end. I looked to Lachlan and he pointed underneath to a cupboard and bending down, I pulled out a piece to mount it to. I walked back over to Cassie.

"On your knees," I told her.

She did as she was told.

I placed it under her.

"Use that to please yourself as you watch us," I whispered to her. "But no coming, not just yet. I want that dildo coated with your juices when I come back to you."

She nodded and lowered herself down onto the dildo. I watched her as she fucked it slowly and it made my dick even harder.

I sank to my knees in front of Rex and took him in my mouth. He ran his hand into my hair and gazed down at me, a look in his eyes that I hadn't seen before, at least not directed at me. It was as close to love that he probably could manage.

I sucked him hard, grazing my teeth down his length, making him suck in a breath.

"Oh, yes," he murmured. "That feels good."

Lachlan joined us now, standing next to Rex and kissing him slowly as I gave him a blow job that was making me long for a lot more. I took hold of Lachlan's cock and jerked him off slowly. I licked Rex's tip and plunged my mouth back over him again.

I heard Cassie panting louder, she was fucking the dildo as if it was one of us and I knew she wanted to come when she stopped and took a deep breath before she carried on.

"Good girl," Lachlan murmured to her. "Keep denying yourself that release. It will be so much sweeter."

"Yes, Daddy," she murmured.

"Are you enjoying watching your men give each other pleasure?" he asked.

"Yes," she panted. "Yes, I want to see more."

She shifted her shoulders, but I didn't go to her to ease her discomfort. Rex drew his cock out of my mouth.

"I don't want to come in your mouth," he rasped, gripping it tightly and masturbating fiercely to keep his arousal high.

I blinked at him and spun around on my knees.

I was shaking. Not even Lachlan and I had gotten this far yet, but it was time to get on with it. Past time, even.

I dropped onto all fours and clenched when I felt Lachlan's hand on my ass.

"Relax," he murmured, and squirted out some lube.

I took in a deep breath and let him touch my asshole. His touch was soft as he lubed me up nice and slippery. I clenched again when he slipped a finger inside me, but again, he murmured, "Relax."

I did. I had to or it was going to hurt way more.

Rex was already on his knees behind me, the slap-slap of him masturbating loud in my ears.

Lachlan knelt next to us and took his growing cock in his hand.

I gulped as I felt Rex's dick at my rear hole. I looked over at Cassie and she was riveted. She was rubbing her clit against the dildo, her mouth parted, her eyes full of raw lust. She licked her lips as her eyes met mine. It was all I needed to breathe out and let Rex guide his cock inside me.

I kept my eyes on Cassie's as she continued to tease her clit on the dildo. "Yes," she moaned. "Yes, please let me come, please."

"Not yet," Lachlan chided her. He was masturbating furiously as Rex shoved his entire length into me and then pulled back and started to fuck my ass.

I groaned, feeling him fill me up in a way that I'd never

imagined could feel so good. He grabbed my hips and thrust in and out a couple of times before he picked up his pace. He pounded into me, and I felt myself coming all over the carpet long before he let go. I groaned as I spurted out jets of cum. Cassie's eyes went to my dick. She moaned and closed her eyes.

"Open your eyes and watch your Master get fucked in his ass," I barked at her.

Her eyes flew open in surprise at my tone and she watched as Rex thrust one last time and then came inside my ass with a loud grunt.

"Fuck," Cassie said, her lips quivering as she held onto her own orgasm. "Fuck!" she roared, letting us know she was over this and wanted out of her chains.

But we weren't done. Or at least, Lachlan wasn't done with me yet. As soon as Rex withdrew, Lachlan was kneeling behind me and slipping his dick inside me.

"Oh, yes, Suits," he murmured. "Oh, I've wanted to fuck your tight ass since the day I met you."

I started to pant as I felt my cock stiffen a little bit. I'd never known it to go up again so quickly. I doubted I would come again any time soon, but it felt so good.

I lowered myself to my elbows and Lachlan drove deeper into me, fucking me roughly.

I enjoyed every single hard thrust and finally let Cassie have her release as I watched her sweating and writhing around on the dildo as if her life depended on it.

"Come now!" I roared at her. "Let your Master see how hard you come around that black cock."

"FUCK!" she cried out. Her whole body shuddered uncontrollably as she sat down on the enormous fake cock and let her orgasm thunder over her at the same time that Lachlan pounded into me and then let go, his cum pumping into my ass to mingle with Rex's and slip back out as he withdrew.

He sat back on the carpet, panting like a racehorse and I

crawled over to Cassie to kiss her, to drag her off the dildo and feel her wet pussy against my palm.

"Good girl," I murmured to her as I ravaged her mouth with my tongue and fucked her wet pussy with my fingers.

I was almost all the way hard when I dragged her onto my lap and guided my cock inside her. She screamed my name as she fucked me hard and without mercy, using all of her strength to pull up on the chains and then slam back down on me. She came within a few seconds, milking me so hard I grunted and felt myself coming already. It was weak, a feeble attempt but it got the job done and I fell back to the carpet with her suspended above me. It was the biggest turn on to see her like that, inked nipples clamped and rock hard, hands chained above her head.

Lachlan released her from the manacles, and she slumped down on top of me. Rex massaged her shoulders quickly as Lachlan picked up the dildo and wiped her cum off it to lube up her ass. I groaned as she leaned forward, and I propped myself up to watch over her shoulder as he inserted it into her.

She cried out at the enormous size of the black cock, but that soon turned to moans of pleasure, especially when Rex started playing with her clit.

"Fuck," I muttered as she came again and then we all flopped back to the carpet to catch our breath and hope that we'd started to move on from that horrendous night.

23

~Rex~

I was curled up next to Cassie, needing to be close to her, but until she said I could touch her, I couldn't, so I lay as close as I could to her.

Several minutes passed as we all took in what just happened.

It was a bit surreal.

I'd known that I was starting to see Alex in a different light. It was the day he'd decided to take up the role that I had abandoned in Cassie's life. It made me look at him in a whole new way and I liked it. I enjoyed seeing him assert himself with her. I'd never expected that I would fuck him so soon. I'd figured we'd take our time, like he and Lachlan had. They were far more in a relationship than we were, but it was the right time and Cassie wanted it.

Seeing her watching us as she fucked the dildo had been purely spectacular. She was a vision.

I let out a soft whimper, needing to touch her.

Lachlan broke up the group first by getting up and walking over to the drawers. He pulled out a packet of hygiene wipes and the key to Cassie's cuffs. He threw the wipes to me first, knowing that I needed to slide my dick into my Mistress as soon as she gave me the go ahead. He bent to uncuff Cassie and rubbed her wrists, kissing them, soothing her.

"Daddy loves you, Princess," he murmured, and I watched as her eyes lit up.

She was so into their chosen roles even after the ordeal with Rob.

"I'm sorry for hurting you."

"I deserved it," she answered softly.

"Do you feel better?"

I waited for her answer. I knew the guilt was eating her up over the other night. I'd tried to save her from that burden, but it was there, nonetheless.

She sighed heavily. "In all honesty, no, but what can we do about it except turn ourselves in?"

"No," I croaked out. "We talked about this the other night, Cassie. If anyone goes down, it's me. No one else. Ruby needs you, and so do they." I gestured to the other two men with my chin.

"*I* need *you*," she whispered.

"Then we stick to the plan," Alex stated with such authority that it was the end of the conversation.

For now.

There was no way that this was the true end of it.

"Mistress?" I asked her cautiously. "I need you."

She sat up immediately, realizing that everyone had the time in their roles, except me. I didn't want to say that I felt hard done by, but I did.

Alex helped her to her feet, and I got to my knees. She slipped her high heels back on and took hold of the flogger that Lachlan handed to her. The two men retreated then to watch. I was fine with that. They both seemed happy to tag team Cassie and dominate her in their different ways, but I didn't want that. All I wanted was Cassie to whip me. She walked behind me.

"Have you been a naughty boy?" she whispered in my ear, leaning her hands on my shoulders.

"Yes."

"I saw you looking at Eliza's tits the other day in the car. Do you want her, puppy?" she bit out sharply.

"What?" I choked out in shock. I hadn't been expecting that.

She hit me with the flogger, and I grunted as the feeling of relief washed over me.

"No," I replied, answering her question. "No, I don't want her. I only want you, Mistress."

She walked around to the front and brushed the flogger over my cock. It stiffened and she sneered at me.

"Are you thinking about her tits now?"

"No," I grit out. I'd never seen this side of her before. She was jealous of the woman that I'd laid eyes on only once. I narrowed my eyes at Lachlan, before looking back into hers. *He* was clearly the target of her actual rage. "I'm thinking about yours. I want to push them together and slide my dick in between them. Will you let me, Mistress, please?"

"Maybe," she said, putting her foot to my chest, shoving me backwards. "Did you like sticking your dick in Alex?" she asked wickedly, twirling the flogger around my cock.

"Yes."

"Did it make you feel good?"

"Yes."

"Do you want to do it again?"

"Yes."

"Do you want him to do it to you?"

"Yes."

"Mmmm," she purred, lowering herself down onto me and smashing her wet pussy against my cock. "I want to see that. I want to suck your cock as he rides your ass. Do you want that, baby?"

"Yes," I whispered.

My dick was so hard now, it was twitching, eager to be

inside her.

She knew it and she climbed off me.

She circled me like a predator and then brought the flogger down on my back. I let out a moan of desire.

"So, so naughty…"

She whipped me again.

"You didn't let me play earlier. You tied me up and made me watch you."

"I'm sorry," I murmured.

We heard a door open and close and I realized that Alex and Lachlan had left us alone. I raised an eyebrow at her as she gave me a slow seductive smile as she lowered herself to my lap again.

"All alone," she whispered, leaning down to brush her clamped nipples against my chest.

My heart thumped. Would she give me alone time? I'd wanted it for so long. Lachlan told me that Alex'd had it and that he'd come close a few days ago.

I reached out to unclamp her nipples. If this was alone time, I didn't want it to be about the roles. I wanted it to be about *us.*

She smiled at me and I sat up to gently suck her nipples. She threw the flogger to the side and gripped my head to her breasts, throwing her head back as she writhed on my lap.

"I want you," I moaned into her perfect tits.

"Take me," she said, and I didn't need asking twice.

I guided my cock into her, and she rode me slowly, as I swirled my tongue around her peaks, my hands clutching at her ass to get her even closer to me.

"I love you," I murmured to her.

"I love you," she replied, pulling my head up so that she could brush her lips against mine.

"Thank you," I breathed.

She giggled. "Don't thank me. I decided we all needed time alone."

I wasn't sure if she meant each of us with her, or with each other as well. I wasn't sure if that was something I would pursue. It would be too intimate and that I reserved only for the woman in my arms, my wife, my Angel, my redemption.

She sped up and rode me hard. I fell back to the carpet and let her use me for her own pleasure. Mine could wait. I wanted her to come and feel fulfilled before I let go of my own tension. I felt her clench around me, and I moaned softly as she cried out, then she did something unexpected. She rolled us over so that I was on top of her.

"Make love to me," she whispered.

I kissed her deeply then and did as she asked, making slow love to her until I was ready to burst.

She came again and I had to let go.

I thrust inside her and then spurted my cum deep into her as I buried myself as far as I could go.

It was the first time that I'd felt true happiness, but it flitted off all too quickly, leaving me feeling cold and alone.

She wrapped her arms around me and stroked my hair.

"You don't ever have to feel that you can't trust me, Rex," she whispered. "I am here for you. Always."

"I know," I said, even though I didn't want to believe her. Even now, after everything, I still didn't want to believe that she loved me in case it all went away and then I would be left with nothing but my darkness. I closed my eyes and saw Suzanne again. She was all I saw when I shut out the world. Her death was plaguing me like no other. Not out of guilt for killing her. She deserved it. She was ready to kill her own child, my love, my *life*, but I felt like I owed her. Without her, Cassie wouldn't exist and for that I would always be grateful to her.

"I'm sorry," I muttered.

"You have nothing to be sorry for," Cassie murmured back, but I wasn't apologizing to her. Not this time anyway. I was apologizing to Suzanne. I owed her my life and yet I'd taken hers away.

That wouldn't sit right with me for a long time to come.

24

~Cassie~

The days rolled by and soon we were meeting with Uncle Teddy to hand Scarlet back to him. We would have done it sooner, but he'd been away. He didn't even attend my mother's funeral.

I stroked her chubby face and she giggled at me. I beamed at her and picked her up from the crib in Ruby's room to give her a cuddle. I'd grown very attached to her, in spite of who her mother was. I knew that Alex felt differently about her now that she wasn't his, but he still loved her. It was hard not to. She was an absolute delight.

"I'm going to miss you," I whispered, holding her close. "But you belong with your daddy now."

The weight that dropped into the pit of my stomach made me feel ill. Rex and Lachlan had told me how they'd found her. Were we sending her back into a horrible situation?

"Ready?" Lachlan asked.

I nodded slowly. He noticed my hesitation but didn't say anything.

As we walked out into the sitting room, I saw Ruby, Alex

and Rex waiting for me and I blurted out, "I want another tattoo!"

"Okay," Alex said, looking puzzled. "Any reason for the sudden exclamation?"

"It's just…" I gulped. How could I tell them? I felt silly now that I'd started to say it out loud.

"What is it?" Rex asked

I felt my cheeks go red as I looked down. "With Rob…he wanted my tattoos removed before he…uhm…you know. I guess, what I'm trying to say is that they saved me, and I want to add to them."

"You have no need to feel embarrassed about that," Lachlan said, giving me a one-armed cuddle. "It's a valid reason."

"If he wasn't already dead," Rex growled, clenching his fists.

"Do you know what you want?" Alex interjected quickly before Rex started punching things.

"Yes," I said with a smile. "I want our initials, down my spine. A, C, L, R, R…and S." I watched for their reaction.

Confused frowns turned to surprise as their eyes went to the baby in my arms.

"What are you saying?" Alex asked slowly.

"I want to keep her," I stated. "We can't in good conscience give her back to Uncle Teddy. She is my family and I want her here, with us."

There was a lengthy pause and I suddenly felt awful for my declaration. I hadn't *asked* them, I'd told them.

"If that's okay with you, of course," I added with a grimace.

Lachlan was the first one to speak. "Of course, it's okay, Cas. I've been feeling like shit about giving her back."

"Me too," Alex said with relief.

Rex took a bit longer, but then I suspected he would. "If that is what you want, then we will make sure that we keep her."

I frowned at him. "That's not a very positive response, Rex."

He frowned back at me. "I don't want her going back there either, okay," he muttered looking away and I grinned at him.

"Better," I said. "We'd better speak to a lawyer before we go there."

"I have a feeling we won't need one," Lachlan mumbled and then ushered us to the elevator. "Let's just go there and say our piece."

I nodded, trusting him. I had absolutely no reason to believe that Uncle Teddy would want Scarlet. I doubted he even knew she was his. But we had to do this regardless, so better to get it over with.

❧❧❧

WE MADE our way to the SUV and I strapped Scarlet into the new seat we'd bought her. Alex put Ruby in on the other side and I smiled at him over the babies. "When all of this is over and Ruby is a little bit older, we'll try."

His eyes went wide and then tears shone before he blinked them back. "Thank you," he whispered and then clambered into the middle. I got into the passenger side, with Lachlan grumbling about being squashed right in the back.

"We need a bigger car," he stated with a huff.

Rex got in and we set off.

"Agreed," I said and then we fell into an easy silence as we contemplated a future with another small baby in it. Scarlet was a bit older than Ruby, so it was going to be a learning curve to catch up with her development, but I realized that I was looking forward to it.

"We also need a bigger house," Rex commented after a few minutes.

I gave him a confused look. "No, the babies can share, and

we've already gotten rid of the playroom. It's not appropriate anymore."

He gripped the steering wheel tighter. "No, we need a bigger house. A house, Cas, in the suburbs, where the children will be safer."

"Oh," I said, understanding where this was coming from. "I love living in the city."

"But *that's* not appropriate anymore. I'm not going to be pushed aside on this. I will keep pursuing this until you give in. So, you might as well just cave now." He gave me a slight side smile that warmed me up in all sorts of places.

"Or I could always get your Master to tell you how it's going to be," he added with a low, dark tone that made me shiver in an incredibly good way. If the babies weren't in the car, he would've been in trouble.

"Oh, will you now," I purred back. "In that case, I refuse to see your point of view."

Alex stifled his snort of amusement and leaned forward between the seats. He ran a fingertip down my neck before his hand circled my throat and he squeezed slightly.

I went damp between my legs.

"Listen to him, sweetheart," he whispered harshly in my ear.

"Yes, Master," I murmured, and he released me and sat back in his seat as if nothing had happened.

Rex was smirking at me. I knew that he was enjoying this. He had a way to control me without having to do it himself. It was the perfect arrangement for him. I wasn't so vain as to think it was *all* about me, though. Having some sort of control over Alex was also a huge turn on for him.

With delicious thoughts dancing in my head, we continued our journey in silence until we pulled up at Uncle Teddy's estate.

Rex pressed the buzzer and we were let in. He drove up to the house and I looked around. I hated my parent's estate which was remarkably similar to this one. I'd never felt comfortable there. I'd never thought Rex would be the one to suggest that we move to a place like this. I do understand his reasoning, though. The girls could play outside and be safe behind the huge walls, secure gates and security at every turn.

I sighed and decided that he was right. We had to make the move soon. "Look into it," I told him as I got out of the car. Then, I looked back in and said to Alex, "The girls really should stay here."

He nodded and settled back in between them as Lachlan grumbled as he climbed out. "You sit back there on the way home."

"Okay, Daddy," I whispered to him and watched his eyes darken.

But then we turned to the house as Uncle Teddy came out all smiles and hugs.

"I was so sorry to hear about your mother," he said insincerely, patting me on the back before pulling away.

He escorted us inside

I nodded grimly. I didn't want to talk about her. Or my father, who had been absent throughout this entire nightmare, unsurprisingly.

"Damien sends his…"

"Don't," I said, interrupting him with my hand up. "I just can't."

He nodded and dropped it. "So, what brings you by?"

I took in a deep breath, noticing that he hadn't even acknowledged Rex or Lachlan since we'd been here. Frosty was the vibe I was getting but didn't question it. Nor did I make mention of the fact that my Uncle made a business out of having people killed for money. I would take that to my grave, not for Teddy's sake, but for Rex's.

"Scarlet," I said and watched closely for a reaction.

His face went cold. "Oh?"

"Do you know who her father is?" I asked tentatively.

He shrugged. "No clue. I'd say ask your mother, but…"

That got my attention momentarily. "Why her?"

"She and Ella met up and were quite the secret pair. I see why now. Obviously, they were plotting against you. I figured maybe she'd known."

"Hmm," I murmured. "Well, actually *I* know," I said and pulled the letter out of my bag that Rex had handed to me a few days earlier.

Teddy raised an eyebrow and looked at it. "And I need to know, why?"

"Just read it," I muttered and shoved it at him.

He did and his face went puce. "Lies!" he spat out. "She obviously fabricated this to get to my money."

"She didn't do that test, I did," Rex said. "I used your DNA and it clearly states that Scarlet is yours."

Teddy's face went furious. "You little shit! I will see you in court for doing this behind my back."

"Calm down," I snapped at him, jumping to my husband's defense. "No one needs to go to court, unless you actually want her?"

"Pah," he spit out. "Pity her mother is dead because I'm not interested."

I tried not to recoil from the sheer coldness of his words. How could he not want his own daughter? I was shocked, but it made this even easier. "*I* want her," I stated. "I trust that you won't fight me for guardianship."

His eyebrows nearly shot off his face. "What?" he spluttered. "You?"

"She is my cousin and I cannot in good conscience hand her over to you to neglect," I spat out.

He chuckled and relaxed. "Take her," he said. "I won't fight you. But if you accept guardianship, you'd better be prepared to accept that fully. I will be renouncing parental rights so that she can never come after me for anything."

"Fantastic," I snarled at him, finally seeing him for who he truly was, an evil monster that took advantage of a lonely, desperate boy who had nothing to live for. "I will have my lawyer draw up the papers. Once you sign them, I never want to see you again. I know who you are now, *Uncle* and I don't like what I see."

I spun on my heel and stormed out of the house with Rex and Lachlan close behind me. I cursed the earth as I climbed awkwardly into the very back seat, leaving Lachlan to slide gracefully into the front. I felt bad for making him sit here. *I* barely fit so he must've been very uncomfortable on the drive over.

"Let's get out of here," I muttered as Rex gunned it out of the driveway, "and do me favor, when you find us a house, make sure it is as far away from him as you can possibly get. I never want Scarlet to know what a hateful man he is."

"Done," Rex muttered.

Alex looked over the seat at me and held his hand out for me to take. "That bad? He's going to fight for her?"

"No, he practically threw her at us. He is awful."

"Oh," he said and looked at her. "Well, *we* want her, and she will be safe and loved and never know that her real father didn't want her."

"Yes," I said, brightening considerably at his words. "She is our family now and she will never feel lost or alone. We will make sure that she never feels like we did growing up."

"Agreed," the men said and for the first time in a while, I felt relaxed and happy that something was going right.

25

~Lachlan~

I rubbed my forehead. The thumping music coming from the dance floor was like a hammer to my head. I didn't normally get headaches, but this one had come out of nowhere and had my head in a vice-like grip.

"Water," I shouted to the barman, who slid it wordlessly across the bar at me.

I gulped it back and slammed the glass down. I turned and sighed. This event was huge. Someone had hired the club out for their own party, and it was packed to capacity. We were turning people away. Eliza had called me two hours ago to help out. I'd been reluctant to leave Cassie and the girls this late on. It was pushing 1.00am now and I wanted to get home.

I hoped the throngs would die down soon so that I could make tracks but so far it wasn't looking likely.

I made my way back across the dance floor, weaving in and out of the gyrating crowd. I needed to make sure that everyone was behaving themselves and I couldn't do that from the sidelines. I had to be in the thick of it.

That's when I got cornered and wished I was anywhere but there.

A pair of hands – not the first ones tonight – slipped around my waist as a woman pushed herself up against my back, hands dropping to my crotch.

"Sorry, I'm married," I started as I grabbed the hands and recognized the black talons immediately.

"Yeah, to an uptight little girl," Eliza laughed in my ear. "Come on, Lach. One little dance, no one will know."

She started to move her hips as I dropped her hands. Gritting my teeth, I stepped away from her. Turning, I said, "Don't ever disrespect Cassie."

She smiled and swept her hands through her long red hair and up over her head, which lifted her tits and made them look even more enticing in the cut-out bra, minus the nipple clamps tonight. She was showing it all off in a completely see-through skirt, made of chiffon or something, with absolutely nothing underneath.

"I'm not disrespecting," she said. "I just want to have some fun. Don't you?"

"Not with you," I stated, turning from her and walked away.

She followed me quickly and pushed me against the wall as we headed into the corridor that led to my office.

Her hands went to my dick again as she whispered, "I want a taste."

"Eliza," I sighed and pushed her gently away. "I'm not interested."

"I could show you a really good time," she purred. "I know what you like."

My head was pounding viciously, and I didn't have the energy to keep arguing with her. I'd never been so happy to see Rex in all my life as he loomed up behind her in that menacing, very sexy way of his. He grabbed her by the arm.

"He's not interested, don't touch him again," he warned.

My dick went hard now. I hadn't been affected by Eliza's touch, but Rex's presence had alerted the officer and he stood to attention.

"Ooh, you're a bad boy, aren't you," she murmured to him, sliding her hands up his chest. He gripped them tightly enough that she yelped and then he shoved her away.

"Are you doing this to piss Cassie off?" he asked her bluntly. "Is this a vendetta? Has she done something to you in the past?"

Eliza stiffened and pulled her hands back. She straightened her back and lifted her chin. "It has nothing to do with Cassie," she stated. "I want some fun, that's all."

"Well, go and find it elsewhere," Rex replied, narrowing his eyes at her, which then dropped lower to take in her body. They lingered on the tattoo that she had on her hip, that was clearly visible as her skirt didn't start until a bit lower.

"Like what you see, after all?" she purred. "I'll let you tie me up and whip me."

"He isn't into that," I snapped, getting pissed off with her come on *and* with Rex checking her out.

"Oh, really?" she asked with an arched eyebrow. "I didn't peg you as a Subbie, bad boy."

"What I am is none of your business," he growled at her.

She giggled. "Ooh, Cassie is one lucky lady. Put in a good word for me with her. I like a bit of girl-on-girl and she is smokin' hot. You wanna see us together, bad boy? I know you do, Lach. I saw it in the car the other day. I would lick her cunt until she screamed in pleasure…"

Rex grabbed my arm and hauled me off to the side, away from Eliza. "Not interested. If I see you sniffing around him again, I will see to it that you regret it. And stay away from Alex, as well," he added almost as an afterthought. "I can guarantee you; he isn't interested in you."

She scowled fiercely at him, which I found a bit odd, but then he practically kicked my ass through my office door and slammed it shut behind us.

"What the fuck?" he grated out. "Leading her on is a bad idea."

"I wasn't," I complained and put my fingers over my eyes. "Fuck, my head…"

"Are you okay?" he asked, instantly full of concern, coming to me and massaging my shoulders.

"If you keep that up, I might not be responsible for my actions," I murmured.

"It's not like you to be sick," he commented, digging his strong fingers into my neck.

I groaned with satisfaction. "Just a headache. This music isn't helping."

"Getting old?" he smirked.

"Ha, speak to Alex about that. I'm still a spring chicken."

"A gorgeous one at that."

I blinked and gave him a curious look. "You coming on to me, bad boy?" I leered.

"Maybe," he said. "Cassie gave us the go ahead to, you know, develop our own relationships."

"I know she did," I replied, vividly remembering the conversation only yesterday where she informed us that if we had a moment to go with it, even if she wasn't there. "Do you think she meant it?"

"You don't?"

I shrugged. "I dunno. It doesn't seem fair somehow."

He nodded and stepped back. "I agree."

"You were testing me?" My anger flared up. "How dare you, fucker." The thumping in my head got worse and my vision went blurry.

"Not testing, just seeing where your head was at," he responded mildly. "Clearly, though, your head is killing you so how about I take you home and we can pick this up with our wife in attendance tomorrow."

"Yeah," I said. "I need to tell Eliza that I'm going."

"I'll tell her," he said shortly. "Go to the car."

I nodded and regretted moving my head. "Yeah," I muttered and took the key from him, stumbling out of the back door to avoid as many people as possible.

"Fuck," I grumbled as I leaned against the car as I opened it. Something wasn't right. I felt like death on a stick. Maybe I was having a migraine. If Alex felt as half as bad as I did right now when he had one, I pitied him even more.

"Get in," Rex said, appearing at my side and helping me.

"Did you speak to Eliza?" I asked, frowning at him. He hadn't been long.

He nodded grimly and I wondered what had bit him on the ass. Hopefully *not* Eliza.

"Can we keep the last half an hour to ourselves?" I ventured as Rex set off. If Cassie heard about Eliza's come-ons, we'd be toast.

"Absolutely," he agreed and then we sat in welcome silence for the rest of the ride home. I could always rely on Rex to be quiet when I needed him to be.

A little while later, Rex got me upstairs and into bed. Cassie was fussing over me, but Alex told her to leave me alone. I was both grateful and pissed off. I wanted my wife hovering over me. But silently hovering, of course.

❦

I woke up to Cassie snuggled in next to me and Alex on the other side. I could hear the babies awake with Rex murmuring to them and I smiled. I felt better. Drained but better.

"Hey," Alex said, waking up as I climbed out of bed. "How're you feeling?"

"Okay," I said with a shrug.

"You looked like shit last night. Have you ever suffered from migraines?"

"Nope, healthy as a horse. Usually."

"Hm," he muttered and gave me a searching look. "Sure you're okay?"

"Just a headache," I assured him, checking my phone. I

had turned it off when I got in last night and there were about a dozen texts from Eliza and a few voicemails.

I frowned and checked the texts. All of them were apologies for coming on to me. She'd gotten the wrong impression of my relationship with Cassie and thought it was a free for all. She didn't realize that we were committed to each other, blah, blah. All the same bullshit we hear every other time someone discovers that Cassie is married to all of us. I ignored them as I didn't have the right mood to deal with it. I was unusually tetchy when I got in the shower and even scowled at Alex as he barged in behind me.

"Sorry, work, you know." He shrugged.

I narrowed my eyes at him and then opened the shower door and bellowed, "Cassie!"

She came running in. "Everything okay?" she exclaimed, looking around frantically.

"Yes, stay right where you are," I instructed her and then looked at Alex. "On your knees, Suits. You know you want to."

He chuckled at me. "Well, if you insist," and he dropped down, the water cascading over me as he gave me a blow job that I definitely needed to ease some of the tension.

I grunted as I finished, my hand on the shower door to steady me.

"I didn't need to be here for that," Cassie murmured. "We talked about this."

"You didn't enjoy it?" I asked archly.

"Of course, I did," she breathed. "I'm just saying…"

"It doesn't feel right to do it without you. Rex feels the same. Suits?" I asked brusquely.

"Agreed," he said and ducked out of the shower, grabbing a towel to dry off.

"Fair enough," she murmured, knowing I was in a mood, and she knew me well enough to know to back off and leave me alone. I hated that I was being a dick, especially to her, but my nerves felt raw.

I needed to speak to Eliza and clear up any confusion that my bumbling around might have caused last night.

I was a no-go area and for good measure so were Cassie, Rex and Alex. If she wanted to mess with us, she was heading for trouble and I would have to find someone else to run the club.

I got out of the shower and quietly got dried and dressed. I slipped out with minimal communication, which further upset my wife. There was no way that I was telling her where I was going and why. She would hit the roof. She must've had Eliza's card from the beginning, and I was a fool to dismiss her concerns.

"Wait up," Rex called as I reached the sidewalk. "We need to talk."

"What about?"

"Eliza," he said and grabbed my arm, steering me away from the building. "She's here to cause trouble and we have to put a stop to it. Today."

26

~Alex~

I sat at work but couldn't concentrate. There was too much going through my head. Not the least of which was my very evolved relationship with both Rex and Lachlan. The other day in the club playroom had changed everything dramatically for all of us. I'd never expected Rex to initiate that kind of move. I knew that we'd had a change in feelings, but it all came on quite suddenly. It was palpable, hot and exciting.

I groaned as my dick went hard.

"Fuck," I muttered and sat back in my chair, spinning around to look out over the city.

A knock at the door interrupted my thoughts. "Yeah?" I called out, turning back around and scooting my chair under the desk as far as I could manage to cover up the bulge in my pants.

"Hey," Cassie said as she poked her head around the door.

"Hi," I replied with a big smile. "What are you doing

here? Not that I'm complaining." I got up to kiss her. She wheeled the double stroller into my office and gave me a huff.

"I wanted to ask you something."

"You could have called," I pointed out as I led her to the small sofa in the corner.

"I'm worried about Lachlan," she said as she sat and slumped forward. "Did you notice how 'off' he was this morning?"

"Yeah. I figured he wasn't feeling too good."

"He doesn't get sick. He's, like, renowned for it. I'm worried. Could you check on him? If I go, he'll get pissy with me like he did this morning." Tears sprang into her eyes. She was really upset about this. I pulled her to me, and she clung to me as she got a hold of herself.

"Sorry," she mumbled, pulling away.

"Don't be," I chided her. "You've been through so much this past year, Cassie. You're allowed to get upset."

She gave me a wan smile and sat back. "My birthday is coming soon. You know what that means. It's weighing on me and after everything that happened…I don't feel that I'm coping very well," she added in a small voice.

"Oh, Cas, you are still so young and you've had so much trauma recently. You don't have to be strong all of the time. You have us to hold you up when you need it."

"I'm not used to being weak," she protested vehemently. "I've always had to look after myself, be strong and fearless."

"You don't have to be that all the time now, my love. If you feel like crying and screaming, do it. Bottling it up will only make it worse."

She nodded, but I wasn't sure if she was taking it in or not. "Will you speak to Lach?"

"Of course." I doubted I would get very far, but I would speak to him anyway.

"Thanks," she muttered and then stood up. She paused and sat back down. "I felt that everything was finally becoming right. I'm scared that something else is going to blow up in our faces. I can't take much more."

"We are going to be fine," I told her firmly. "We have had enough trouble to last us several lifetimes. It can go looking for someone else now, it's had its fun with us." I smiled at her and she giggled.

"I hope you're right. I need normal."

I nodded. "Uhm, have you had alone time with Lachlan yet?" I ventured.

She shook her head.

"Maybe find the time later. He knows about us and you and Rex. He's probably feeling left out, that's all." I didn't know if that was true, but it made her smile as it gave her something she could resolve.

"Definitely. Would you and Rex take the babies later?"

"Of course."

"I'd better go. George is being extra tetchy lately with our security. He wanted to come in, but I told him to stay outside the door. He wasn't impressed."

I grinned, picturing George's stern face. No, I doubted that he was impressed at all by Cassie's demand.

"Be safe, love," I whispered to her, giving her a kiss.

She left my office with a brighter smile than when she entered it.

I sighed and decided that I had to get back to work.

My phone buzzed on my desk, so I walked over to pick it up. I scowled at it and threw it back down. I wasn't in the mood to deal with that particular problem right now. It turned my disposition sour and I snapped at Lachlan and Rex when they came to see me a little while after Cassie left.

"What is it?" I barked out.

"Err, we need to talk," Lachlan said, closing the door behind him.

"What about? You? Cassie is worried, sort it out."

He frowned at me.

"Sorry," I mumbled, "I didn't mean for that to come out

that way. She came by to see me just now and she *is* worried about you. Is it because you haven't had one-on-one with her?"

He huffed. "Well, thanks for rubbing that in," he gritted out. "But no, I know it'll come. Right now, we have a bigger issue."

I exhaled and sat back down. "Hit me," I sighed.

"Not here. You might start yelling," Lachlan said.

"What do you mean?" I frowned deeply at him, giving myself a headache. "What have you done?"

"Just come with us," he said.

"I can't, I'm at work," I pointed out.

"Take an early lunch," he insisted.

"Fine," I grumbled and called my assistant to tell her I was stepping out. I was concerned with what this was about. Why would they be worried *I* would start yelling? It had to be something to do with me and that wasn't good. I had no more secrets – that I knew of anyway – so I racked my brain to think what this could be about.

I gulped and asked with dread, "Am I in trouble with the police? Did they find some trace of me at the hotel?"

"No! Nothing like that," Lachlan reassured me, but looking at Rex's grim face, I wasn't assured at all that I wasn't in trouble. "We've debated this point all morning, but Rex won, so here we are."

"Where are we going?" I asked as no one said another word when they ushered me out of my office and down to the lobby.

Rex was double parked, so we hurried to get in the SUV.

"This is show, not tell," Rex clipped out.

My stomach dropped. "Is...is Ella still alive?" I whispered.

"No!" Lachlan exclaimed. "Just be quiet and you will see shortly."

I chewed the inside of my cheek and remained silent for the rest of the ride. They said nothing either.

I was in full blown anxiety mode when we pulled up

outside *Corsets & Collars*. I had no clue what we were doing here. The suspense was killing me.

As we got out of the SUV, Lachlan took me by the hand and led us inside. "Just so you know, I had no idea. Absolutely no idea."

"About what?" I asked, perplexed.

"That," he said and pointed over to the bar.

I blinked once, twice and then scowled so fiercely my face felt like it was going to explode.

A woman with vivid red hair in waves down her back, dressed in practically nothing except a pair of nipple clamps and a see-through skirt, stalked out from behind the bar.

The wicked glint in her eyes made me shudder as she walked right up to us and purred in that voice that made my skin crawl. "Hey, little bro. Glad to see me?"

27

~Cassie~

I was excited about tonight. Even though I'd said that I didn't want it planned out, just for it to be spontaneous, this was different. Lachlan needed me and I wanted to give him a perfect night as we had never had sex just the two of us before. It was going to be a bit weird, but also thrilling. I'd booked us a hotel room, *not* the Four Seasons, so that the babies could stay here with Alex and Rex, but Lachlan and I had time to be with each other with no interruptions and no play. I didn't want that, and I was assuming he wouldn't either.

I looked at the clock and it was after lunch time. I thought that he would be back by now after he stormed out of here this morning. I hadn't even spoken to him.

I picked up my phone and deliberated for a second before I unlocked it and scrolled over to the tracking app. I didn't want to use it. I had *never* used it as I hadn't felt the need to be *that* woman, but right now, the feeling in the pit of my stomach made me push it and click on his name. I watched as the circle blinked a few times and then homed in on his phone…at Coco.

Well, I supposed that made sense. I didn't see anything untoward about that, in spite of sexy Eliza slinking around in her BDSM outfits that made me wildly jealous. It had been too long since I'd dressed up and made my men drool.

I gulped when I remembered the last time. It had been the night that Rob abducted me. I shuddered but pushed it aside. I didn't want to think about that ever again.

"Aurora?" I called out, heading into the nursery.

She looked up at me from the floor where she was playing with the girls. She was a godsend. Truly. She took on the extra responsibility with no complaints whatsoever, only delight.

"I'm going to run an errand," I told her. "Will you be okay for a while?"

She rolled her eyes at me in mock exasperation. "Of course," she said. "Go. We will be here having fun when you get back. Or maybe some of us will be sleeping, tired out from all this play."

I giggled. "Perfect. Uhm, stay locked up tight, don't go anywhere. Ted and Jeff will be right outside the front door and I'll lock the elevator from up here."

She nodded, taking this instruction for the gazillionth time in just a few short days as seriously as the first time.

"And remember, if there is a fire…"

"Head up to the roof and call your grandfather who will send the helicopter right away. Got it," she said with a smile.

I breathed out in relief. "Sorry," I said. "I know you've got this."

"We'll be fine," she said, standing up and squeezing my hands. "Go and run your errand. I'll call you in half an hour."

I nodded and headed out, locking the elevator and then heading to the front door.

Ted and Jeff nodded at me as I passed, calling George to meet me downstairs. Jeff stepped into the elevator with me and I smiled hesitantly at him. He was sterner than George and that was saying something.

He saw me to the curb where George took over.

I was just about to slide into the Mercedes when someone calling my name, made me pause.

"Ms. Bellingham?"

I turned. George was already stepping in front of me, but I recognized the man instantly and my blood ran cold.

"Detective Winstanley," I said steadily. "What can I do for you?"

"Is your husband home? I need to speak to him," he said brusquely.

"Which one?" I asked lightly, trying not to show my fear.

His pudgy face gave me a disgusted look as he raked his gaze over me, making me feel dirty. He looked at his notebook, even though I knew it was a ruse. He knew who he was here for.

"Rex Black," he stated. "He at home?"

"No," I said, shaking my head. "Can I take a message?"

"Tell him to call me," he said, holding out a business card.

George snatched it from him with a fierce look.

The Detective, used to hardened criminals, didn't even flinch.

It made me nervous. Very, very nervous.

"Will do," I chirped and cursed myself as I sounded so false. He was bound to suspect I was hiding everything to do with his case.

George ushered me closer to the car and I slid in as quickly as I could without it being obvious.

"It's in his best interests to call me," the Detective called out as George slammed the door shut.

I nodded grimly and then George was pulling away from the curb as the Detective stood staring after us.

My hands were shaking as I pulled out my phone. I called Rex immediately.

He answered on the second ring. "Everything okay with you and the girls?" he said quietly.

I nodded, even though he couldn't see me, and recited

what he'd told me to say if everything was okay. "Yes, the girls are fine. So am I."

"Good," he said. "I'll call you back in five minutes."

Then he hung up.

I gaped at the phone in shock that he'd done that. What could be so important that he dismissed me in favor of whatever it was?

I shoved my phone into my jacket pocket with a clenched jaw. Asshole.

I would be at the club in five minutes.

A thought occurred to me and I pulled my phone back out, scrolling to the locator app again. I clicked on Rex and it let me know that he was also at Coco.

I grimaced. What were those two up to?

It belatedly occurred to me that maybe they were spending some quality time together. Although, they had both told me that they didn't want to engage with each other without me there, maybe the moment came over them. I wouldn't begrudge them that but seeing as George was already pulling up to CoCo, I had to go in now.

"I'll be around the back," he said as he let me out and saw me to the door, which Stan opened and then escorted me inside.

"Thanks," I muttered and giving Stan a smile, I headed off to find my husbands.

I did *not* expect to also find Alex as I strolled into the bar area, sitting at the counter with...I had to blink twice to make sure that I wasn't imagining it. Eliza. She was wearing his fucking suit jacket, looking as sexy as fuck in Armani and fuck all else by the looks of it.

I felt my face go puce as I stormed over to him, only seeing Lachlan and Rex out of the corner of my eye, skulking off to the side. They both leapt forward as they saw me bull-dozing my way through the thin crowd of people to grip Eliza by the arm.

I hauled her off the bar stool. "Not satisfied with just

going after Lachlan, you skanky ho, now you want Alex as well?" I shrieked, causing a scene I would later be so embarrassed about.

"It's not what you think!" Alex exclaimed, getting in between the two of us. "Let me explain."

"Move," I told him, that one word so cold, he actually did as I asked.

"Cas, wait," he said, taking me gently by my arm and turning me towards him. "It really isn't what you think. She's my sister."

Silence had descended as everyone in the club had turned to watch the spectacle I was causing. I felt my cheeks flame.

"What?" I spluttered. "Your sister?"

"In the flesh, sugar," Eliza said, cocking her hip and holding her hands up.

"Fuck," I muttered and then grabbed Alex's hands. "I'm sorry… I don't know what came over me. It's been an anxious few minutes…it's no excuse…."

"Hey," he said, taking my face in his hands. "It's okay. What do you mean 'an anxious few minutes'?"

"I'll explain later," I muttered.

I turned back to Eliza with an apologetic look. "I'm sorry for overreacting."

"No worries, baby," she laughed. "You weren't all wrong. If Lachlan had been up for it, I would've gone there. Rex too," she added slyly.

I went apoplectic!

I got in her face, my fist clenched, ready to punch the shit out of this husband stealer, whether she was my sister-in-law or not.

"Kidding," she said, still laughing, holding her hands up. "Although…maybe not. You have got some hot guys flocking you, baby. What's your secret?"

"Beth," Alex snapped at her. "Shut the fuck up."

"Beth?" I asked, shaking my head.

She held out her hand, introductory style. "Elizabeth Harris, at your service."

"Harris?"

"I took my mother's name," she said as Alex muttered, "I took my father's name."

"Ooh," I said, nodding like I understood, but my mind was reeling from this information overload. "Shall we go somewhere more private to talk?" I asked.

"Nothing else to say," Alex said shortly. "Beth is packing her bags and getting the fuck out of here. Tonight."

"What?" I asked, frowning at him. I knew he didn't get on with this mother or sister, so much so that he cut them out of his life, but she was here in front of him.

"She used Lachlan and this club to get to me, to get to *you* and your money. Don't trust a word she says," he spat out.

"Al, come on, little brother. I explained already…"

"Save it for someone who cares," he snapped, and turned on his heel and marched out, leaving me and Eliza – Beth – to look at each other as *the* most uncomfortable silence I'd ever encountered descended upon us.

28

~Rex~

We stood there for a few minutes in an awkward silence. Cassie turned her eyes to me, and I shrugged. I knew what she was thinking so I said, "I realized last night. Told Lachlan this morning and we told Alex a few hours ago."

"You realized?" she squinted at me.

I went close to her and said, "Remember Jerry?"

She nodded and gulped at the mention of my old pimp.

"She worked for him too."

"Oh," she said and left it at that. "Uhm, I suppose we should…" She jutted her thumb out.

"Yeah," I said and without saying anything to Eliza, I swept Cassie out of CoCo and back into the Mercedes with instructions to George to go straight home.

"Wait, what about you two?" she asked.

"We'll meet you there," I said and closed the door, banging on the roof to get George to go.

I spun as Lachlan came up behind me. "That went terribly," he said.

"Yeah, but it had to be done. So, have you fired her yet?"

"No, I don't think I want to. I mean, okay, it's weird that she's Alex's sister but she is damn good at this job."

"He isn't going to like having her around."

"So, he doesn't have to see her. Simple. If we ever come here, he can avoid her."

I rolled my eyes at him. "If the tables were turned, how would you feel?"

"Why are you so eager to defend him all of a sudden?" he snapped at me in a completely un-Lachlan way.

"Because I care about him," I snapped back. "You are being completely unreasonable."

"Oh, you *care* about him now, do you. Well, fuck you. Fuck both of you." He stormed off back into the club as I stared after him.

"What the fuck?" I muttered, wondering if I should go after him or leave it.

In the end, I went after him. He was acting way too weird for me not to find out what was going on with him.

I found him in his office, looking grimly through the books. "What's bitten you on the ass?" I demanded, folding my arms across my chest.

He gave me a cursory glance before he went back to scowling at the books.

I didn't think he was going to speak when he finally muttered, "That event last night. I think someone drugged me. No idea who or why, but we have got a serious fucking problem with security in this place."

"What?" I asked with a frown. This *was* a serious fucking problem. First Cassie now Lachlan.

"Rob *is* dead, isn't he?" he blurted out.

Slightly taken aback, I snapped at him. "Yes, of course. Do you think I would let him live after what he did to my wife?"

"I just…" He pinched the bridge of his nose. "Why me?"

"Why not you? You're a hot piece of ass that is completely

unavailable in a place like this. You are like the forbidden fruit."

"You think I'm a hot piece of ass?" he smirked at me, more like his old self.

"Mm-hm," I murmured. "We should go. Cassie'll be waiting for us."

"I need to go back to the security camera recordings. I have to see what the fuck happened and when and by whom. It doesn't make sense, no matter what your take is on it."

"If I leave you here with Eliza, Cassie will have my balls for dinner. You're coming. View the recordings from home."

"With Cassie there? No way. I'm not telling her this. Not after what she went through."

"I'll keep her busy," I told him.

"Like fuck," he responded. "Both you and Alex have had alone time with her. Neither of you get it again without my turn first."

"I didn't mean that," I chided him. "Come now. She'll be worried."

He knew I was right, so he capitulated and followed me out, texting as he went. I knew he was messaging Eliza, but I said nothing. It was business. That was it.

❧❧❧

BACK IN THE CAR, we were quiet.

"Why do you think Cassie called you earlier?" he asked as we pulled into the parking garage of the apartment building.

"I don't know." It had been bothering me the whole way home. She wouldn't have called for no reason. She wasn't like that.

"Hmm," he muttered and then sighed.

"Hey," I said to him. He turned to me and I cupped his face. "I know that I haven't said this before, but I love you, Lachlan. I need you."

He blinked once and then grinned at me. "About fucking time, Angelwings. Make a guy wait forever, why don't you."

I smirked at him and leaned forward to kiss him softly.

"Don't," he said, pulling back. "I want more than just a stolen kiss after you say those words."

"I want to…" I murmured. "I doubt Cassie will be in the mood though."

He unzipped his pants and took his dick in his hand. He started to pump, and I watched him, turning with a quizzical look. "What are you doing? We can't."

"I'm masturbating and you are watching. There's no harm in that."

I accepted his reasoning because I really wanted to watch him.

"You're fucking sexy," I whispered to him.

He groaned and pumped harder. "More," he panted.

I leaned closer. "I want to feel your dick in my ass as Alex sucks me off."

"Fuuuuuck," he moaned at that visual.

I smiled darkly. I had never been into dirty talk. I'd never had to be. There wasn't a woman that I'd fucked that hadn't dropped her panties for me, wanting me because I was a dark soul, they thought they could fix. Even with Cassie, we'd never needed dirty talk. We craved each other and it was enough. There was absolutely no reason for it now, Lachlan would come for me regardless, but having that power to make him harder, to make him moan and pant and have his dick seep out precum because of words I'd spoken was intoxicating.

"Tighten your hand. Pretend you're inside me. Pound me hard, Lach, I want it. I want you to punish my ass."

"Jesus," he cried, doing as I asked.

"Fuck, I want to taste your cum," I whispered.

"Do it," he cried out. "Please!"

"I want it so bad."

"Rex!" he cried.

He shuddered and came as I closed my hand over his tip to catch it.

"You utter bastard," he panted with a laugh.

I brought my hand to my mouth and licked it clean causing him to grunt, the lust clear in his eyes.

"You taste so good," I told him as I climbed out of the car, leaving him to zip up and follow me.

"I'll repay the favor," he muttered to me as he pushed the button for the private elevator.

"Can't wait," I replied, but then stabbed the button again. "Cassie must've locked it."

He nodded and in a companionable silence we headed for the main elevator and stood side-by-side as we went up to the top.

♥♥♥

WE FOUND Cassie feeding Ruby as we entered the penthouse.

"Alex is at Finn's," she said by way of a greeting. "Go to him. We'll be fine."

Lachlan and I exchanged a look.

"What?" she asked when she caught it.

"Nothing," Lachlan sighed and bent down to kiss her.

"Later, you and me and no one else," she whispered to him.

He grinned at her. "About time."

I kissed her as well, wondering if she could taste Lachlan in my mouth.

She gave me a coy look, that I couldn't read, but decided that she probably knew something had happened. She didn't seem upset and while it hadn't been fucking, it had been a sexual moment between us that had excluded her and was only about us. I didn't feel as guilty about that as I thought I would. Lachlan didn't either. Perhaps there was a gray area where we could play, but not fuck.

"We'll see you in a bit," I said to her.

"Not too late. I have plans that I don't want that woman ruining."

"Plans?" Lachlan chirped. "Lucky me."

"You will be," she laughed and then shooed us out.

We went and found Alex down the street in Finn's bar, sitting in a booth with an untouched beer in front of him.

29

~Alex~

I could not believe that my sister was here and had inserted herself into Lachlan's club to get to me. Yes, I'd been ignoring her calls for months now, but for good reason. She was a grifter. Always had been. Now she saw that I was married to Cassie, and she wanted a piece of it. Well, it wasn't going to happen. She could fuck off before I gave her a penny.

"Hey," Lachlan said, and he slid into the booth next to me and Rex sat opposite.

"Go away," I muttered.

"Look, I honestly didn't know, I swear. Her background check was clean."

"I believe you," I said, "but doesn't change the fact that I've been successfully ignoring her for ages and now she's here."

"Sorry," he said. "But she's a great club manager. She really cares about the girls. I don't want to lose her."

I caught Rex's eyes and he looked grim. Well, grimmer than usual.

"What do you know?" I sighed.

"Remember that day that you saw me at your place?"

I nodded. How could I forget?

"That wasn't the first time I'd been there. A few days previous to that, I'd been there. When I was…finished…Jerry told me to go outside and wait in the car while he and your mom settled up. I walked through the house and saw Eliza in the sitting room with two guys. They were treating her pretty rough, but I didn't want to butt in. I went outside and she joined me a few minutes later for a smoke. We spoke briefly, found solace for a moment in each other that we were both victims of Jerry, but she was strong, Alex, really strong. She showed me her tattoo, the one on her hip of the phoenix. She told me that she would die in that life but rise again to make a new one. It stuck with me, you know. It gave me the courage to run when you told me to, to get out and make my own way."

I gulped and felt goosebumps. To learn that my sister was a prostitute under the same pimp as Rex was gut wrenching. The fact that my mother knew about it, probably enforced it, was something that I just couldn't deal with.

"What do you mean you found solace with each other?" I asked quietly.

"Do you want me to spell it out?" he asked back.

"Jesus," I muttered and stifled the retch. This was too much.

"She wants to make amends," Lachlan said. "She's really upset."

"That's what she wants you to think," I spat out. "I don't believe a word of it." But there was a part of me that now felt bad. I'd had no clue what she was going through growing up. She shielded me from the horror of knowing that she was being abused and that our mother liked to tie up innocent young boys, whip them and fuck them in the basement.

"She's dead," I blurted out.

They gave me curious looks. "Our mother. Beth told me that she'd died of cancer over a year ago. Right around the time that Cassie and I first met. She called me on her death bed, and I ignored her."

"Fuck," Lachlan murmured. "Sorry, man."

I gave him an incredulous look. "I'm not. She was a monster."

He gave me a look that said he agreed with me, so I knew his words were just platitudes. Something you say to someone whose mother died.

"Eliza was a victim," he said quietly. "You can't blame her for that."

"She could have left! She is three years older than me, she could've gone and never looked back!"

"And that would've left you," Rex whispered to me, leaning forward and taking my hand. "Your mother was the one who had the arrangement with Jerry for the money. If Eliza hadn't been there, then..." He paused and a haunted look that I hadn't seen for a while crossed his face. "Trust me when I say that Jerry was not concerned whether his assets were male or female."

I shuddered and my stomach churned. "She protected me."

He squeezed my hand, but I pulled away and shoved Lachlan out of the booth. I stumbled into the men's room and threw up the entire contents of my stomach into the toilet as they slunk in behind me.

"Don't let it get to you," Rex said, which was easy for him to say. He was the king of tortured souls. "She did what she had to do to protect you. That was *her* choice. Don't blame her for it and don't punish her. Take what she is offering now and move on from it."

I flushed the toilet and nodded because he was right.

We had a lot to talk about, a long road in front of us, but if I didn't try to fix this mess between us, *I* was the dick.

"Let's go home," Lachlan said and took Rex's hand as he let me wash my face and rinse my mouth out.

I squinted at them in the mirror. "Something I should

know about?" They had a different vibe; it was like electricity sparking between them.

They looked at each other with a secret smile and I felt left out. Hurt.

"We may have found a murky area," Lachlan said, turning back to me. "Perhaps something that we can all agree on."

"What do you mean?" I asked.

"Fun but without fucking," Rex said.

"What? You two alone?" I asked, incredulous and a bit jealous.

"Don't be jealous, Suits," Lachlan laughed. "Rex has a fantasy and let me tell you, he is damn good with the words."

"Oh," I said slowly, getting it. "He talks, you act?"

"Something like that."

"Cassie know yet?"

"Not yet, she sent us here before we could say anything."

I nodded. "Thanks for coming."

"Always," Rex said.

Coming from him, that one word meant everything.

"Didn't peg you for a man of pretty words," I said as we left the men's room and headed out of the bar.

"Oh, Suits," Lachlan sighed. "He can make a man come with a few sentences."

I chuckled. "Look forward to finding out."

"Me too," Rex said darkly, but there was a heat in his eyes that fired up my own lust. Too bad Cassie wanted Lachlan to herself later, but maybe Rex and I could put this new arrangement to the test. *If* Cassie gave us her approval.

30

~Cassie~

I looked at the clock. I'd bathed and fed both babies, so they were settled happily now. I was anxiously awaiting the return of my men. I suspected they wouldn't be long.

I pondered while I waited, the connection that I'd seen between Rex and Lachlan earlier. It was different, emotionally heightened, sexually deeper. They'd been up to something alone and that was fine. I'd wanted it, but they all disagreed with me. I didn't see it as a betrayal. If they went off with another woman, well, that would be the ultimate treachery, but I was one hundred percent sure that they wouldn't. I may have felt jealous of Eliza, but that was *my* issue, not theirs. I was jealous that she got to live her life out in the open, be who she wanted to be and was free to do whatever the hell she wanted. Don't get me wrong. I loved my daughter more than anything else in this life. I adored Scarlet as if she was my own. But even before my children, my husbands, I had *never* been able to be who I wanted out in the open. There was expectation and family and the business. The Bellingham Legacy.

My wandering thoughts were brought back down as the men came in, happy and together.

"Hey," I said lightly. "Everything okay?"

"Yes," Alex said, coming over to give me a kiss. "They put me straight on a few things. I need to speak to Beth, try and sort out this shitstorm."

I nodded. I'd expected that he would. "Good," I said and then looked past him to the two who looked like they needed to say something.

I smiled at them, taking Alex's hand and leading him over to the sofa. "Got something on your minds?" I asked them.

"Actually, yes," Lachlan said and went into a long-winded explanation which was completely unnecessary, but I let him get it out the way he wanted to. I *did* raise my eyebrow when he said that Rex could talk dirty like a pro but I stayed silent. I would put that to the test myself one day soon.

"Perfect," I said when he finished. "I'm glad that you have found something you are happy with." I wanted to ask them to record it now and again so that I could watch it back, but that kind of defeated the purpose of it being "theirs". I supposed it was the same as them asking me to record the one-on-ones so the others could watch.

They grinned at me and I was happy. I almost forgot about the Detective that showed up, but that will be tomorrow's problem. Right now, I had something to say before I took Lachlan away and we spent some alone time together.

"Rex," I said, and he looked up at me in question. "I know that you didn't really get your Sub time the other day. I know it's something that you need, so we'll do it soon, okay?"

He just nodded, but I saw the look of relief in his eyes. He needed it and I'd been terrible for not giving it to him.

I leaned forward to kiss him, digging my sharp nails into the back of his neck as I drew him close.

His soft groan was muffled by my mouth and I deepened the kiss.

I pulled away to murmur at his lips, "Be a good boy while I'm gone."

"Yes, Mistress," he whispered back, his eyes closed.

I smiled and kissed him again, then it was time to leave with Lachlan. My nerves were frazzled, but I was excited at the same time.

We left them silently by the front door. It seemed to be preferable, leaving the elevator locked, especially at nighttime.

I'd already alerted George, so he was waiting for us with the Mercedes and we slid into the back.

"The Towers," I muttered to him and he set off.

"You okay?" Lachlan asked after a beat.

I nodded with a smile. "Yes. Uhm, I want to be back before Alex goes to sleep, is that okay?"

He gave me a look that made me feel a bit dumb for asking. "Of course. I don't want any of us to be apart."

"It only gives us a couple of hours…"

"It's enough," he interrupted me, taking my hands and kissing them. "You didn't need to do this."

"I know, but I was very aware that time was ticking on without our time together."

He smiled at me and I snuggled into him, enjoying the quiet for a minute.

"I love you," I said suddenly, sitting back up and taking his face in my hands. "I really love you."

He chuckled. "It sounds strange coming from you with no one else here. It's perfect. It's everything I ever wanted. Since the moment I first saw you, I knew you were special, Cassandra. I love you completely."

I grinned at him and settled back down, cuddling him, my hand on his thigh. After a while I said, "I'm glad that the three of you are taking matters further on your own."

"It's a little strange, but after he told me that he loved me, I couldn't help myself."

I sat up again, surprised. This was the first I'd heard of that. "He said that?" I croaked out.

He nodded. "Don't be concerned, Sweetcheeks. He doesn't love me the same way that he loves you. He has grown to care about me because I love him and he knows that I'm there for him, no matter what. I—I will take it at face value."

"Do you love him the same as you love me?" I asked in a small voice. I hated to ask, but since he sort of brought it up…

He gave me a puzzled frown. "No, absolutely not, Cas. I've loved you forever, you are my world, my everything. I would give up everything else just to be with you, including him."

I gave him a relieved smile. "Luckily, I'm not asking you to," I said lightly and snuggled into him again.

"Thank fuck," he chortled. "I am a 'have my cake and eat it too' man."

"With a cherry on top," I agreed, also with a laugh. "I do love you all so much. Seeing you together…mmm."

"Stop it," he murmured to me, moving my hand further up his thigh until he reached his cock. "You are going to make me do things in front of George that he probably wouldn't appreciate."

George snorted and I bit my lip. I wouldn't be opposed to that. Having someone watch you have sex was the biggest turn on.

"No," Lachlan spluttered as I gave him a look. "This night is for you and me, no one else."

"Later then," I told him, and he shook his head at me in exasperation.

Not a few minutes later, we were climbing out of the car at the hotel telling George to come back at 10.30pm. It gave us a few hours to be alone before we went back and became a group again.

I was dying to know if Alex and Rex would do something while we were gone. I was betting that Lachlan was thinking the same, but after we checked in and tumbled into the room, clinging to each other, I focused on Lachlan.

He swept me up into his arms, kissing me as I wrapped my legs around him. He shoved me up against the wall, his hands going to my shirt to unbutton and pull off.

He groaned as he latched onto my nipples through the lacy fabric of my bra.

I struggled with his t-shirt, finally getting it up over his head, exposing his ripped abs to me that I had to run my hands down.

"So gorgeous," I murmured as he unclasped my bra.

He spun us around and dropped me onto the bed, taking my shoes off and as I unzipped my jeans.

He dragged them off me and moaned in appreciation as he found me without underwear.

He was quick to strip off the rest of his clothes and then he was on me, thrusting deep inside as I wrapped my legs around him again, lifting my hips and arching my back.

"Fuck, yes," he muttered. "All to myself."

"Yes," I cried out as he slammed into me.

Even without foreplay, I was dripping wet for him. He turned me on just by being him. They all did.

I ran my hands up his arms as he braced himself over me, pounding into me until I came with a fire of lust burning through me. I clenched around him hard and he grunted, pulling out and flipping me over. He pulled me up so that I was on all fours and he drove back inside my slippery pussy, pumping his hips in short bursts that drove me wild. I came again as he switched it up and thrust long and hard.

"Oh!" I screamed as my arms gave way and I pressed my cheek against the sheets, driving my ass higher.

"Fuck, Cas," he groaned, feeling me clutch his cock again and again. "I'd always fantasized what that would feel like and it surpasses my wildest dreams."

"Lach," I cried out as he relentlessly pumped and pumped.

He pulled out again right when I was about to come again, and I screamed in frustration as he chuckled at me. "So desperate for my cock, aren't you?"

"Oh, yes," I moaned as he spun me around, sitting back and pulling me onto his lap.

"Ride me hard, baby," he whispered.

He guided his dick back inside me and I gripped his shoulders, using every muscle that I had to ride him like a fucking cowgirl on her last day on this green earth. I wanted him to come, I wanted him undone.

"No chance," he panted, knowing my thoughts somehow. "I want you in every position I can get you in before I let go."

"Damn you!" I cried, speeding up even more.

"If I come now, I'm out for more than a few minutes," he pointed out.

"You have a mouth and fingers, don't you?" I retorted to his amusement.

"Sorry, baby, but this dick needs to be inside you for as long as possible," he panted and pulled me off him again, turning me around and putting me back on his dick reverse cowgirl style.

He fingered my clit, pinching it and rolling it around as I worked hard over him, exhausting myself. I slumped back against him, but it was worth it. I came in an explosion of fireworks and something so unexpected happened, we both froze momentarily. I squirted for the first time during sex.

"Jesus," Lachlan moaned, as I covered his hand in juices, and that seemed to be his undoing.

He flooded me in an orgasm that shuddered through his body, his cock jerking wildly as he spurted stream after stream of cum into me.

"Oh, Cas, you are amazing," he whispered into my ear. "That is the sexiest thing that I've ever seen."

I giggled. "You *can't* tell the other two. They'll be jealous."

"Oh, you have got to be kidding me," he whined. "I was about to plaster it all over social media."

"Ah!" I cried, horrified that he might just do that. "No!"

He laughed and took me off his cock. He placed me gently down, curling up around me.

"I have to tell them," he murmured to me.

"Fine," I huffed. "But don't brag about it."

"Take away my accomplishment, why don't you?" he snorted.

I giggled and failed to point out that it wasn't so much *him* as me. Although, I suppose he had a large part in it. I rolled onto my front and he propped himself up on his elbow, tracing his fingers down my spine.

"Here," he said. "For your new tattoo."

I nodded, feeling too sleepy to reply with words.

"I'll get one too," he added.

I turned my head towards him to regard him thoughtfully. "Yeah?"

"It's a gesture."

"A very nice one."

"Rex will too. So, Alex will have no choice."

"I like it. It will connect us forever and ever."

He lightly kissed my nose as he scooted down to lie next to me. "Are you ready for round two?"

I snorted. "Are *you*?" I grabbed his cock, and it wasn't anywhere near ready enough in my opinion.

"As you so succinctly pointed out, I have a mouth and fingers," he waggled the latter at me. "So, on your back, Princess, Daddy wants to tongue fuck you til you scream."

"Oh, fuuuuck," I groaned and did as he ordered.

Much screaming later, when he was ready to slide into me, we made sweet love until we had to get up and get showered to go back home, even closer for the time we had just spent with each other.

31

~Rex~

Alex and I hadn't made much conversation since Cassie and Lachlan left us. I was preoccupied with searching for a new house and he appeared to be working on his laptop. I'd made myself comfortable on the sofa in just a pair of black sweats, which sort of matched what he was wearing, except he had a black t-shirt on as well.

Annoyingly.

I'd have preferred to check him out while his nose was stuck in his work. I'd given *him* the chance to check me out. Where was the reciprocation?

I went back to searching. William had sent over a few properties that he thought would be suitable, but they were all on Long Island. I was sure without even asking her, that Cassie wouldn't appreciate the commute. I'd found a couple in Westchester which I thought she might go for.

I felt Alex's eyes on me and looked up. He stood up and came closer, taking his t-shirt off as he came closer.

"Felt it was fair," he said.

I slammed my laptop shut and threw it next to me on the

160

sofa. He wanted to do something, and I was game for whatever he had in mind.

"What do you want to do?" I asked him quietly.

"I want to touch your angel wings," he murmured, his eyes on my lower abdomen.

I raised an eyebrow at him. "Touching isn't really on the table."

He lowered himself to his knees and my breath caught as his hands hovered over me. "Just once," he murmured.

I pulled my sweats down a bit more to show them off to him fully. His eyes went darker and he placed his hands flat out on the tattoos and then drew his thumbs over them. His touch was light, warm, soft and it made my dick stir.

"When I saw you in the gym, before we knew each other, I thought you were a god. Now, I *know* it," he whispered.

I put my hands over his and without thinking moved them lower. His eyes hooded as he pulled my sweats right down so that my cock sprang free.

"I want to touch you," he said.

"You can't," I replied, but took myself in my hand and started to jerk off with his eyes on me. "Do you want me to come on your face?"

"Yes," he croaked out; his eyes riveted to my hand wrapped around my length.

"Tell me what you will do to Cassie next time we play."

"I want to blindfold her, tie her up and flog her. I want to bite her nipples until she screams and make her fuck the handle of the flogger until she comes all over it."

"Uhn," I groaned and pumped harder. "More."

"I will masturbate in front of her, not allowing her to touch me, and then come all over her tits. I want to fuck her in her ass with the dildo, I want to keep my dick away from her until she begs me for it."

"Jesus," I muttered. I got now why Lachlan was so turned on earlier. Dirty talk was hot. I closed my eyes and let my head fall back as he murmured all of the things he wanted to do to her, things that he probably would never do but was just saying it to turn me on.

"I want her bound up so tight as we take turns fucking her," he said and that was it. I burst my banks, spurting my cum on his face as I opened my eyes to see it happening.

"Yes," I muttered. "I want that too."

It surprised me that Alex had even thought about it, never mind said it out loud. But I also knew that Cassie would agree to it. She would get off on it.

"Shibari," I said quietly. "She'd love it."

He gave me a quizzical look as he reached for the box of tissues. "I'll look into it," he said and stood up as the front door opened to let in Cassie and Lachlan.

They looked at my dick still out and Alex wiping his face and grinned.

"Have fun?" Cassie asked, kicking her shoes off.

"Did you?" Alex returned.

"Oh, yeah, but I think my little pet needs a spanking now," she said darkly.

I was on my knees in the next second, head lowered as my Mistress stalked me in her bare feet.

"Want us to stay?" Lachlan asked quietly.

"You can go and get me the collar from the bedroom, along with the flogger and the nipple clamp. This puppy has been really naughty."

I was thrilled at her words. She was going to give me exactly what I craved, what I needed to maintain normal human behavior and not deep dive off the cliff that I stood on every second of every day.

"I've been so bad," I muttered.

"Oh, you're going to get punished, my darling, don't you worry about that."

Lachlan returned with the items she'd asked for and I dropped onto all fours so that she could attach the collar around my neck.

"Take his pants off," she instructed, and he did as she asked, stripping me naked. "Now leave."

"Yes, ma'am," Lachlan murmured, and took Alex away, leaving me to be whipped to my heart's desire.

She was harsh with me, almost cruel and it made me want to weep with relief. She teased me, flogged me, gently whipped my cock until I wanted to come but she wouldn't let me. She clamped my nipples and, upon my suggestion that I'd stolen from Alex, she fucked my ass with the flogger handle, using her own cum as lube. She made me lick her pussy until she flooded my mouth with her sweet nectar and then she sucked my cock, giving me no mercy.

It was the most magnificent night of my life.

As she led me by my collar to the bedroom, to finish the job on our white cloud of a bed, I fell even more in love with her if that was possible.

She opened her legs wide as her other men ravaged her and I sank into her as she kept hold of my leash, tugging on it tightly so that I'd fuck her harder.

"My Angel," I murmured as her pussy clenched fiercely around my cock.

"My Dark Angel," she replied, and it was the three words that not even a pack of wild dogs could stop the force of the orgasm that came over me.

I unloaded my cum into her pussy, groaning with the sheer release that she'd denied me for over an hour.

I slumped onto her, but I wasn't done yet. Lachlan had taken control and I knew exactly what he wanted to do to me.

As Cassie watched, he fucked my ass as Alex sucked my cock, and then they swapped, using me for their own pleasure until I was able to come again, but they left that honor to my Mistress.

I came in her mouth as she sucked me like a lollipop and finally, finally I felt liberated from the torment that weighed so heavy on my soul.

For now.

32

~Cassie~

I sat at the breakfast bar the next morning with my coffee, happy that yesterday went so well for all of my men. I felt that we were turning a corner with our relationships, but I was worried about this cop problem. I had to tell Rex today.

"Hey," he said, coming out of the second bathroom. He'd just had a shower and he was wet and gorgeous with just a towel slung around his hips.

"Hey," I said softly as he kissed the top of my head and went for the coffee.

"Thank you for last night," he whispered to me, pulling me close once he'd gotten a cup.

"Don't thank me," I chided him. "I love you."

"And I adore you."

I grinned at him as Lachlan and Alex came out, both dressed and ready for the day, like I was.

"So, I have big news," Lachlan said with a smirk at me.

"No!" I exclaimed, hiding my face with a smile.

"Our Princess squirted last night, all over my hand. Fuck, it was hot."

"Nooo," I groaned, but I didn't really mind him telling.

"What?" The other two men gaped at me and I sat serenely giving them a slow smile.

"You two had better up your game," I told them to their delight.

"Challenge accepted," Alex said, bending to kiss me.

I kissed him back briefly, but then took the card that was under my cup and handed it to Rex. "He came by yesterday looking for you," I said seriously, and the light mood went south.

"Did he say why?" he asked stiffly.

"No, just said to tell you it was in your best interests to call him."

"Huh," Rex said and turned to walk back to the bedroom.

"You can't call him!" I blurted out.

"Why not?" he asked, turning back around.

I jumped off the stool and crossed over to him quickly, flinging my arms around him. "I can't lose you," I muttered.

"You will never lose me, Cassie. Never. You and the girls are stuck with me," he said with a soft smile as he brushed my hair out of my face. "And those two clowns as well." He gestured to the other men.

"I'm scared," I murmured. "Please don't call him."

"I have to, or he will keep showing up here. If he was going to arrest me, he'd have come back already."

I knew he was being practical, but it left me feeling cold to my core.

"Please," I begged him.

"Does he have anything?" Lachlan asked before Rex could answer.

"Not a thing. I scrubbed everything and hacked the video after we left. We're good, I promise you," Rex said, but then his eyes went shrewd and he turned them to Lachlan. "Speaking of video recordings...did you find out who drugged you?"

"WHAT?" I roared and turned on my other husband, who flinched from me, but then went violent on Rex.

"You fucker! You had no right to tell her that!"

"Oh, I had every right. No more secrets, remember?"

"Oh, so she knows about you and Eliza then?" Lachlan snarled and I nearly threw up as I looked back at Rex.

"It was a long time ago, before I even knew you." He brushed it off and that seemed to be the end of it. Too bad it wasn't. He was going to have to do way better than that.

Later.

I faced Lachlan, who was grim faced. "You were drugged?"

"The other night?" Alex piped up, also in the dark, apparently. "When you came home sick?"

"Yeah," he said. "I think so. I dunno really."

"You do," Rex said. "So, video?"

"I haven't exactly had time," he pointed out, hands on hips.

"No time like the present," Rex said, folding his arms across his huge chest, which made him look intimidating even if he *was* only wearing a white fluffy towel.

"Humph," Lachlan muttered rudely, but was saved by Aurora bursting through the door, her cheeks red from rushing.

"I'm so sorry for just barging in…" Her eyes went straight to Rex and widened as her flushed cheeks went even redder. "I—I, oh…" She turned around and I couldn't help the smile.

"Go get dressed," I chuckled to him, even though I was still pissed off about the Eliza reveal and worried about the cop thing and now Lachlan's drugging. What was going on? Was the universe against us? It sure fucking felt like it on days like today.

Rex slunk off and I asked Aurora, "Everything okay?"

"No," she said, turning back around, her features under control now. I didn't resent her for it. Rex was gorgeous when he was *clothed*. Half naked, he was enough to make any woman lose her shit. I know, I did.

She faced Lachlan. "You need to come to the club right now. Stan has Becky in lock down. She is…" She twirled her hand at the side of her head.

"What do you mean?" he asked with a frown. "What's happened."

"She is like some crazy-ass stalker. You are her target. Stan caught a glimpse of her locker before she slammed it shut earlier and it was covered in pictures of you. Like, really stalkery ones. You on your own, you and Cassie, you and Rex…it was…" She shook her head.

"Cassie?" Rex barked out, making us all jump as he strode back into the kitchen, now fully clothed.

Aurora nodded and debated for a few seconds whether to come clean or not. I guessed Rex's follow-up growl convinced her to. "Uhm, yeah. There was a picture of the two of you, your eyes were cut out," she said to me, with an apologetic look.

"Oh," I said, a little bit stunned. "I don't even know this girl."

"Yeah, I don't think you are the main focus of her obsession," Aurora pointed out.

"Jesus," Lachlan said and sighed. "Okay, call Stan, tell him I'm coming now."

She nodded.

"I'll come with," Alex said. "I need to speak to Beth anyway. She there?" he added to Aurora.

"Who's Beth?" she asked, looking up from her phone.

"Oh, Eliza," Alex muttered and got a confirmation nod in return as Aurora started talking to Stan.

"I can't cope," I uttered under my breath.

"Hey," Rex said, taking me in his arms. "Everything will be okay."

"Okay," I said, wanting to believe him, but, how could I? Our lives were endangered *again,* and I felt helpless.

"Do you think she was the one that drugged you?" Rex asked Lachlan.

He shrugged as Aurora waved her hand at us and hung up.

"Drugged?"

"Roofie'd," Rex clarified for Lachlan.

"Uh, yeah, Stan found something in her locker. I didn't know what it was."

"Fuck it!" Lachlan kicked out at the stool I'd just been sitting on and it went flying. "This is the last fucking thing I need. If word gets out about this, I'm SUNK!" He slammed his fist on the counter making me jump again. It was very unlike him to be so edgy. Alex put a hand on his shoulder, and it seemed to calm him down enough to mutter an apology.

"We'd better go and sort this out," Alex said. "Cas, we'll call you later."

I nodded a bit dumbstruck. "Okay," I managed to croak out as they left without a kiss or a goodbye.

"I'll get going as well," Rex said. "I will be fine," he added at my fearful look.

I took it on the chin and attempted some strength. "Maybe with *him*. You are in for some serious discipline when you get home for failing to mention you fucked Eliza."

His eyes went dark with desire, but he smirked at me as Aurora's gasp of shock resounded through the kitchen.

"I told you it was a long time ago," he said again, probably more for her benefit than mine.

"Still, puppy has been bad," I murmured as he swooped in to kiss me.

"So bad," he agreed and then he was gone.

Aurora was looking down when I turned back to her. She bit the inside of her cheek and went bright red.

"What?" I asked her.

"Uhm, you and Rex. He likes it?"

"Likes what?" I teased her with a smile.

"You know, you disciplining him, you being his, uhm, Mistress, and all."

"He does. Very much so. Is it something you want with Stan?"

"He wants to try it!" she blurted out. "I don't even know where to start." She covered her face with her hands.

"Don't be embarrassed," I told her, taking her hands and pulling them away from her face. "I can show you a bit of play for beginners."

"Okay," she croaked out and then cleared her throat. "You are going to work today?"

I accepted the change of subject and said, "Yes. My birthday is around the corner and I have to get back to it. It breaks my heart to leave the girls, but at the same time, I'm excited."

"Well, I am here for you, no matter what," she said, back to her old strong self.

"I'm glad," I said, giving her a hug. "Which reminds me. Rex emailed me some properties last night. We're going to be moving to the suburbs pretty soon. I wanted to ask you if you'd move in with us. I mean, not into the house, obviously, you'd have your own place in the grounds and your hours wouldn't change or anything, but I just thought with the commute and… stuff…" I was rambling and hadn't even discussed this with the men yet. But I didn't want to lose her, and I wanted to know that she was safe with us. "Stan too, of course…"

She was gaping at me.

I'd gone too far.

"Just think about it, no need to give me an answer right now," I told her.

"I don't need to think about it," she said with a smile. "I love you guys and I'm honored. Thank you. I'll talk to Stan."

"Great!" I exclaimed, relieved that I hadn't just made a fool of myself. "We love you too."

She beamed at me and then said, "Off you go then, I've

got this. Fire, roof, grandfather, helicopter. Security by front door. No letting anyone in or going out."

I giggled. "Sorry, I know it's a lot."

"It's fine," she reassured me. "Things'll be better in the new house."

"Here's hoping," I said and after going to kiss the girls goodbye, I left to head into work and make sure that everyone knew the boss was back full time and about to start kicking asses.

33

~Lachlan~

I was fuming. I could barely think straight.

"Why?" I roared at Becky as I stormed into Coco with Alex trailing behind me. "Why did you do it?"

"Do what?" she asked casually, which further incensed me, if that was possible.

I glared at her for a moment. She was sitting on a chair with Stan standing over her, a pair of fluffy cuffs round her wrists.

I looked at Stan in disgust.

"It was all I could find in the moment," he answered my glare with a shrug.

"I haven't done anything wrong," Becky pouted those ruby red lips at me, flicking her dark hair over her shoulder. It was only then that I saw she was wearing it the same way Cassie did, in long, raven waves around her shoulders. It used to be lighter and straighter.

I marched up to her and bunched her hair up in my fist, roughly turning her head to see what I *knew* would be there. A pair of angel wings inked on the back of her neck.

"You are sick," I spat at her, releasing her.

"It's what you like," she said.

"No, I like them on my wife," I informed her. "Are you stalking her?"

"No! I don't care about her. This has *nothing* to do with *her*," she scoffed.

The relief was there. At least Cassie was safe.

"I love you, Lach. We can be together."

"Are you fucking delusional?" I shouted at her.

"Why? She cheats on you all the time, right under your fucking nose! You don't seem to care about that, neither does she. Why shouldn't you get to have other women?"

"That's not the way it works!" I yelled, giving myself a headache. "She doesn't cheat on me. We are all in a committed relationship."

"Yeah, keep telling yourself that," her voice full of scorn. "I see it for what it is."

"No, you really have no idea. You are sitting there judging our relationship without a fucking clue how it works. I'm not even going to lower myself into explaining it to your pathetic ass. Why did you drug me?" I asked the question as calmly as I could. Although it was starting to be pretty obvious, I wanted to hear it.

"I wanted to loosen you up so that you'd have some fun with me. But Eliza got to you first. Lucky bitch. What do they have that I don't?" she demanded.

"For starters, Eliza didn't get me. Second of all, *my wife* is the love of my life, she always has been. I would die for her; do you get that? Do you get how much I feel for her? I wouldn't touch you or any other woman with a barge pole because I would never hurt her. Drug me, hold a fucking gun to my head, shoot me…it will *never* happen."

"She doesn't give any of that back to you. I could, Lachlan. I would die for you; I know I would."

I paused, rubbing my hand over my face. "You still don't get it, but you know what, that's fine. You can think about it from your jail cell."

"What?" she asked, paling. "J-jail?"

"You stalked me and drugged me without my consent. Yeah, I'm going to make sure that they throw the book at you. Stan?"

He knew what I wanted him to do and pulled out his phone to ring the police. Yeah, it stung a bit because we were trying to lay low, but this was...*unforgivable* in my eyes. Anyone who tried to get between me and Cassie was going down, in one way or another. Only Rex and Alex got to stake a claim on me other than my wife and if she ever asked us to stop, I would without a shadow of a doubt. We all would. She was our everything.

I spun on my heel and stalked past a silent Alex and disappeared down the hallway to my office. He followed me as I knew he would.

"Don't you want to speak to Eliza?" I asked him.

"In a minute. Just want to make sure you're okay."

"I'm fine," I told him. "Go and sort your family stuff out. I'll be here when you're finished."

"You're sure?" he asked.

I nodded. "It isn't the first time one of the girls has gotten a little crazy, won't be the last. Some of them are a bit damaged, that's why they come here, looking for a better life than being on the pole. But they see me as some benevolent figure that helps them, and feelings get confused. It's the first time I've been drugged though," I added with a frown.

"I get it," he said, and I was sure that he did.

It was a harsh way to look at some of my employees as most of them were good girls, but they'd been dealt a shitty hand. Some of them had started out as prostitutes or strippers and had gotten tired of that life so they came here looking for more. They got it. I was happy to give it to them, to give them a chance at a better life. Some of them hadn't ever been in the lifestyle until they came here, but most of the girls had, as my clientele were the elite of New York and they came here looking for their precise needs to be met. Some of them needed experienced women who knew what they were doing every second of their encounter. But some of them were happy to be handed a beginner who would rather be spanked by a Judge in a safe environment than fucked by a john on the side of the road. The experienced women were the stable ones who enjoyed this and wanted it as part of their life. To the others, like Becky, it was just a job that they went home from.

I sighed. "What a fucking day."

I sat down and stared blankly at the pile of mail on my desk.

I picked up the phone and called Cassie. I didn't want to speak to anyone except her right now. I hated that everyone seemed to think that our relationship was either filthy and disgusting or inconsequential and a bit of fun before Cassie decided to choose one of us and settle down. I didn't know which one was worse. Today? Maybe the latter after Becky's bigoted ravings.

She answered on the second ring. "Hey, Daddy," she purred down the phone and I groaned.

"You have no idea how much I needed to hear that," I told her and relaxed completely as she talked dirty to me on her way to an executive meeting. It might've just been me, but that thought made it even hotter.

34

~Alex~

I left Lachlan reluctantly. If I hadn't come here to speak to Beth, then I wouldn't have left. He was seriously pissed, but something worse. I'd never seen him look so defeated. We'd been through hell more than once and he always seemed to be the one to hold it together better. But today it must've all got too much for him. There was only one person who could fix it and it wasn't me. I hoped that he'd called Cassie the moment I left his office.

I found Beth cleaning up one of the playrooms. She was dressed in short denim shorts and a white t-shirt that was knotted at the front, a bandanna around her head.

"Hey," she said, putting down the enormous dildo she'd been cleaning and dropping the sanitizing spray next to it.

I couldn't help but focus on the rubber gloves she was pulling off as the better option.

"Hey," I said. "You okay?"

She snorted. "Do you care?"

"Of course," I said stiffly and then an awkward silence fell.

She stared at me and I stared at her, neither one of us daring to break it.

In the end, it was me. I was the one that came looking for her. It was my responsibility to surge forward.

"Lachlan makes you clean?" I blurted out and then cursed myself as my cheeks went red and she chuckled.

"No, but the busy work helps me retain some focus, plus I also know it's done right," she said.

I nodded. "You heard about Becky?"

Her face went furious. "Yeah. I knew there was something off about her, I just couldn't put my finger on it. He okay?"

"He'll live," I said.

"Did Rex fill you in?" she asked, looking away.

"He did. Beth…" I gave her a sorrowful look.

"Did he tell you everything?" she interrupted.

"Yes. *Everything*," I emphasized, so she knew I came with all the information.

"He told you that bit?" she asked, surprised, but then she sighed. "It was nothing. A quick fuck to make us feel better about being abused. Does Cassie know?" Her voice went up slightly as she asked that.

"Yeah, she knows."

"Is she pissed?"

"She knows it happened a long time ago. She'll understand, as long as you stay the fuck away from him now. Lachlan as well."

"I didn't know that Rex was that kid until he confronted me the other night," she said as if that explained it away.

"But you knew who Lachlan was. You knew he was married to Cassie and that I was too."

"Yeah, it was hard not to know. It was big talk in this world. Lachlan is a bit of a catch…*was* a bit of a catch."

"*Was* being the very correct word there. Don't try it on with him, you will get burned. He is fiercely loyal to Cassie and I will take his side if I ever hear about you coming on to him again."

She held her hands up. "Noted," she said. "But you don't have to worry. I get the message, loud and clear. I just...I didn't mean any harm...I just..."

"What?" I asked as she stopped.

"Wanted what she has," she replied in a small voice. "I wanted, still want, to be adored by three men who love only me. Hell, *one* man would cut it, but I seem incapable of holding onto one. I'm fucked up, I know it, but as much as I try, I either go too much or not enough. I can't figure it out. I thought that if I got close enough to Lachlan, or Cassie, I could see how they do it."

I sighed. "Relationships take work. Especially ours. There is no easy way out, Beth."

"Eliza, please," she whispered. "Beth is dead."

I nodded, accepting that. "I'm sorry that I didn't see what was happening."

"No! Don't apologize for something you couldn't fix." She gave me a fierce glare. "It's over."

"I will help you in any way that I can, Eliza. I just need to know that you're serious about it," I said, feeling terrible but I *had* to say it.

"I got out. I've made a life for myself and I'm working on the rest. I don't want your money, Alex. Or Cassie's. Lachlan pays well and I've got a lot saved up. I just want you and me to be good. That's all. That's why I came here, to see if we could take a stab at a normal brother/sister relationship."

"I'd like that," I said, stepping closer and taking her in my arms.

She clung to me and I wished that I could really help her, but there was nothing that I could say or do that would take away the pain and horror that our mother had inflicted on her. "If you need anything, I'll try and help you," I murmured to her.

She laughed sadly. "You know what, I'm okay. I'll never be normal, but I've found an outlet here, doing this work.

Please don't let Lachlan fire me." She chewed her lip, looking alone and scared in that moment.

"Are you joking? *He* told me that he wasn't letting you go, and it was tough if I had a problem with it," I said with a smile.

"Do you?" she asked fearfully.

"No," I said, shaking my head. "This is your life, Eliza. I'm not going to stand in the way of that."

"Thanks," she muttered, looking at her feet.

"Uhm, it's Cassie's twenty-fifth birthday next week. There's a small thing at her grandparents' house...I'd like it if you came."

"Aren't her grandparents, like, bajillionaires, or something?" she asked, her eyebrows raised.

I chuckled. "Or something," I said. "They are super nice, though, I know they'd love to meet you."

She looked down at herself. "I'll try and find something appropriate to wear," she snorted. "But thanks, I'd love to, as long as Cassie is okay with it."

"She will be," I told her firmly.

"So, twenty-five, huh? She's still a baby," she snorted.

I laughed. "Don't ever let her hear you say that. But, yeah, I do feel old compared to them sometimes."

"I'm sure you can keep up," she smirked.

I blushed bright red at that, which only made her laugh harder.

"I have no filter, little brother. Sure you still want me to come next week?"

"Yes," I said, "but try not to shock William and Ruby too much, please."

"Promise," she said, holding her hand over her heart.

We exchanged a smile.

"So, I've already met Scarlet, when do I get to meet my other niece?" she asked, and I loved that she accepted that they were mine.

"Soon," I promised. "I'll give you a call."

She nodded. "I should get back to work before Lachlan decides not to keep me around anymore."

I kissed the top of her head and said goodbye, leaving her to it as I made my way back to Lachlan's office.

"You seem in a better mood," I commented as I walked inside without knocking and shut the door behind me.

"Our wife has a way with words," he said smugly.

"Oh, that she does," I agreed. I couldn't help but notice the raging hard-on he was sporting. I leaned on his desk, my eyes on his.

He gave me a questioning look.

"How about we try some of that gray area?" I murmured. "You can tell me everything our wife said."

He sat back, relaxed and happy, unzipping his pants to my delight, as he said, "Well, first things, she was in the office and she wasn't wearing any underwear…"

I groaned and closed my eyes, picturing it perfectly, as his words made me stir.

35

~Cassie~

My hands were shaking as I saw Rex's name flash up on my phone. I answered it, excusing myself from my meeting quite rudely, but I had to know what was going on. Was this his one phone call?

"Hey," he said before I even said anything. "I'm okay before you ask."

"Thank God," I muttered, clutching the phone. "What did he want?"

"Not now. I'll explain everything back at home."

"But you, we, are okay?" I pressed.

"Yeah."

He hung up and I cursed his taciturn ways. "Damn you, Rex," I muttered as I made my way back inside the conference room.

I couldn't concentrate. I just nodded in all the right places and hoped that Marjorie was taking down a comprehensive set of minutes for me to catch up on. I suspected she was. She was good like that. My mind wandered to Alex. I knew that Lachlan was okay, frustrated with all the shit we were taking right now, but he would bounce back. I hoped that Alex and Eliza sorted their stuff out. God knew we were lacking in the extended family department. It would be nice for the girls to have an Auntie that they could go to, like I used to with my Aunt Rebecca before she died.

That sad thought brought Uncle Teddy to my mind. I hated what he'd become. I knew it had to be because of what happened to his wife. That kind of trauma changes a person, makes you do shit you wouldn't have imagined before. But it doesn't excuse his behavior in any way, especially with regards to Rex and of course, Scarlet. I'm disgusted that he could've used Rex the way he did and to disown his own daughter was the final straw. I wanted nothing to do with him now. He and my father could both fuck off and I'd be happy to never see them again.

"Cassie?" Marjorie said gently and I drew my focus to her.

Everyone was looking at me. I cleared my throat. Marjorie made a slashing motion at her neck, signifying it was time to close the meeting.

"Great!" I chirped with a bright smile. "This was fantastic. I look forward to catching up fully and being back at the helm."

I'd pulled it out of my ass, but it worked.

I waited until everyone had left and then let the smile fall from my face. "Thanks," I muttered to Marjorie.

"No worries, honey. I got you."

I gave her a quick smile and then snatched up my phone to call Alex.

"Hey," he panted, startling me. He sounded like he'd run ten miles. "Hang on."

I stalked back into my office while I heard muffled sounds and then he came back on the line as I shut my office door and leaned against it.

"What are you doing?" I asked him suspiciously.

"Helping Lachlan," he said and that's all before he added. "Have you heard from Rex? We can't reach him."

"Yeah, he called a while ago. He said everything's fine with us, but he does have something to say. But how are things with Eliza?"

"Oh, good," he said. "We cleared the air. I invited her to your birthday thing next week. Hope that's okay?"

"Of course," I said with a smile, picturing my grandparents' faces if Eliza showed up in a BDSM outfit.

"Don't worry, she knows to wear something appropriate," he added with a laugh.

I giggled. "Good. Are you on your way home?"

"Lach is. I have to get into work."

"Okay. See you soon," I said, and we hung up.

I pushed off from the door and sat down at my desk. I was itching to get back home, but I needed to stay here for a bit longer to steer this ship in the right direction.

❦

I FINALLY GOT HOME, four hours later to Rex and Lachlan, sitting grim faced on the sofa, staring at nothing.

"What?" I gulped. "What is it?"

"Who the fuck knows?" Lachlan exclaimed. "He won't say anything until you and Alex are home."

"I don't like repeating myself, although I seem to be saying *that* a million times," Rex snarled.

"Alex is on his way," I told them. "I spoke to him about ten minutes ago."

"Then, we wait," Rex said and got up to at least give me a kiss hello.

I gave him a weak smile, but he grabbed my chin and pressed his lips to mine, pushing his tongue into my mouth. I clung to him, needing to feel his strong arms around me and it reassured me. If we were going down, he wouldn't be so calm and loving.

Fortunately, Alex wasn't far behind me, bursting in the front door and throwing his briefcase down.

"What did I miss?" he asked.

"Absolutely nothing," Lachlan groused.

Rex chuckled and led me to the sofa to sit down. "I've already said, we're fine. We aren't implicated in this mess. Teddy is."

"What?" I blurted out. "Why him? And why did they want to speak to you?"

Alex came closer and sat on the coffee table in front of me as I wedged myself between Rex and Lachlan.

"Basically, they were surveilling him and saw us at his place when we went to confront him about Scarlet. As I was the one that Detective Winstanley spoke to after the day at the hotel, he came to me. It could've been any one of us. So, it turns out that the guy who shot Ella worked for Teddy. She managed to turn him onto her side somehow. Anyway, they didn't say much, but I managed to piece it together, by knowing what I know. It seems that Teddy is struggling for money now since his murder for hire business went south when I retired. He took out an insurance policy on Ella which would've seen him straight if she was killed or died of natural causes. They figure the guy who shot her was hired by Teddy to do the deed."

"But what about him, the other guy, Derek and m—my mother?" I asked quietly.

"As we made them believe, Suzanne and Derek were there following a lead on Ella. They suspect that Teddy shot them as they have no other suspect, no gun, no bullets…no evidence of anyone else there."

"No bullets?" I asked in confusion. "How?"

He gave me a look. "Do you really want to know?"

I gulped, keeping my eyes on his. "Yes," I whispered.

"Teddy got rid of them. He knows people. The evidence disappeared after the autopsies."

"He did it to protect us?"

"Yeah," Rex said.

"And we're just going to throw him under the bus?" I balked at the idea.

"It's him or us."

"What if he turns on us?"

"He won't. You think he's gonna stick around and wait to be arrested? He's gone, love. He'll have hit the runway as soon as he got the evidence removed."

I frowned. "Are you sure?"

"Yes, I went to his place before. All locked up, but this was delivered shortly after I got home." He leaned over and picked up a large envelope from the coffee table.

I took it with a shaky hand and opened it. "Oh," I gasped. It was a legal document handing over legal parental rights to me and the men.

"This might come back up in the future," Rex warned us gravely. "But for now, it means that Teddy has given us time until he figures out something else when it comes to that. He might've turned into a monster, Cassie, but he wasn't always that way. He cares about you. I know that. He will protect you."

"Shit," I muttered, putting the envelope and document back on the coffee table. "So, what now? We just go on with our lives waiting for the other shoe to drop? I can't live like that." I covered my face with my hands. "It's no way for the girls to live either."

"I don't think that the other shoe is going to drop," Rex reassured me. "But *if* it does, Teddy will have it in hand. Don't worry, Cassie."

"How can you be so confident?" I asked him.

"Because of this…" he said and held out his phone.

I took it from him and looked at the message from an

unknown number. It said: *I got you, kid. Consider it me owing you. Keep my girls safe. The Captain.*

"Jesus," I whispered and let the tears fall down my cheeks, as Lachlan took the phone from me to read and then handed it to Alex. I had no business hating him when he was doing this for us.

"So, it's over?" I dared to ask. "For us?"

"Yeah," he said. "It's over for us."

"Fuck," Lachlan said, handing the phone back to Rex.

"Yeah," he said again.

"I guess all that's left is to get over the guilt that night has caused," I muttered.

"It's a start," Rex said. "But we had no choice."

I nodded because deep down I knew that, but it was going to take my heart a lot longer to accept it.

❦

WE WENT to bed that night in a somber mood. We didn't really have anything to say to each other after that information overload.

It had taken me ages to get to sleep but when I'd woken, I'd felt lighter than when I'd finally drifted off.

I stood in the nursery early the next morning, and looked at my girls sleeping so soundly, and I knew that we had to make the most of the life that Teddy had given back to us.

I was turning twenty-five next week and it was the day that Grandaddy was going to hand over the rest of my trust to me. The legacy that would eventually go to my babies for them to continue and pass on to theirs.

"How're you feeling?" Alex murmured to me, coming up behind me and wrapping his arms around me.

"I'm okay," I said and turned to face him. "I have to be for these two."

He smiled at me. "It's as good a reason as any."

"Better," I said and grabbed his hand, leading him out of

the room and into the kitchen, where Rex and Lachlan were sipping coffee.

I accepted a cup from Rex and said, "I've decided on a house. The one with the separate cottage on the grounds. For Aurora and Stan."

"Good choice," he said. "I'll make them an offer."

"No," I said, shaking my head. "Give them full price today, and whatever else they need to move out this week. I want to move in as soon as we can."

"Done," he said, hiding his smile behind his cup.

I grinned and looked around the kitchen, filled with my men who I loved so much. I was lucky enough that they loved me back as much. I would be so lost without them. They held me up, gave me the strength to carry on during the worst times and walked by my side during the good times.

I looked at Rex and put my coffee cup down. "Now, who's been a bad puppy?" I asked darkly.

"Me," he answered immediately, lowering his eyes.

"Drop to your knees so that my Daddy and my Master can watch me punish you before they have their wicked ways with me."

He did as I asked without question.

I knew that I would look back one day to this very moment. This moment when I realized that I had everything that I'd ever wanted. A perfect family unit that I couldn't wait to expand on, that gave me so much love, happiness and comfort. It was all any of us ever wanted. I just happened to be the lucky one who had it given to me three times over with three vastly different men.

I couldn't wait to see what our future held. It was exciting and thrilling. Even though I knew that I would have my dark days in the years to come, I was okay with that because I knew my men would never let me fall, and I also knew that I would be there to catch them if they did.

The End

Join my Facebook Reader Group for more info on my latest books and backlist: Forever Eve's Reader Group

Join my newsletter for exclusive news, giveaways and competitions: http://eepurl.com/bxilBT

ABOUT THE AUTHOR

Eve is a British novelist with a specialty for paranormal romance, with strong female leads, causing her to develop a Reverse Harem Fantasy series, several years ago: The Forever Series.

She lives in the UK, with her husband and four kids, so finding the time to write is short, but definitely sweet. She currently has two on-going series, with a number of spin-offs in the making. Eve hopes to release some new and exciting projects in the next couple of years, so stay tuned!

Start Eve's Reverse Harem Fantasy Series, with the first two books in the Forever Series as a double edition!

Newsletter Sign up for exclusive content and giveaways:
http://eepurl.com/bxilBT

Facebook Reader Group:
https://www.facebook.com/groups/ForeverEves

Facebook: http://facebook.com/evenewtonforever

Twitter: https://twitter.com/AuthorEve

Website: https://evenewtonauthor.com/

ALSO BY EVE NEWTON

The Forever Series:

Forever & The Power of One: Double Edition

Revelations

Choices

The Ties That Bind

Trials

Switch & The Other Switch

Secrets

Betrayal

Sacrifice

Conflict & Obsession: Double Edition

Wrath

Revenge

Changes & Forever After: Double Edition

Arathia

Constantine

The Dragon Heiress (Delinda's Story)

The Dark Fae Princess (Savannah's Story)

The Dragon Realms Series:

The Dragon Heiress

Claiming the Throne

A Baby Dragon for Christmas

The Dark Fae Kingdom Series:

The Dark Fae Princess

Dark Fae's Desires

Dark Fae's Secrets

Enchained Hearts Series:

Lives Entwined

Lives Entangled

Lives Endangered

The Bound Series:

Demon Bound

Demon Freed

Demon Returned

Demon Queen Series:

Hell's Belle

Circle of Darkness:

Wild Hearts: Book One

Savage Love: Book Two

Tainted Blood: Book Three

Dark Hearts - A Prequel

Darkest Desires: Book Four

The Early Years Series:

Aefre & Constantine 1 & 2

Printed in Great Britain
by Amazon

75374538R00116